RESURRECTION: AFTERMATH

THE DARK CORNER UNIVERSE
BOOK 10

DAVID W. ADAMS

ISBN:
978-1-916582-31-6 [Paperback]
978-1-916582-32-3 [eBook]
978-1-916582-33-0 [Hardcover]

Copyright © 2023 David W Adams. All rights reserved.

This book is a work of fiction. Names, characters, places, and incidents are either the product of the authors imagination or are used fictitiously or in reference. Any resemblance to persons living, dead or undead, or locales are purely coincidental.

No parts of this book may be reproduced or used in any manner without written permission of the copyright owner except for the use of quotations in book reviews.

CONTENTS

Note From The Author	v
Prologue	1
Chapter 1	7
Chapter 2	15
Chapter 3	21
Chapter 4	35
Chapter 5	43
Chapter 6	51
Chapter 7	57
Chapter 8	61
Chapter 9	67
Chapter 10	71
Chapter 11	75
Chapter 12	79
Chapter 13	85
Chapter 14	89
Chapter 15	93

BONUS CONTENT

Saltair and Krenik's Day Off	99
Acknowledgments	105
About the Author	111

NOTE FROM THE AUTHOR

Firstly, I would like to thank you for picking up a copy of this revised, reformatted, and brand spanking new version of a *Dark Corner* book. I will never take that for granted and appreciate each and every one of you for doing so.

Let's cut to the chase.

This is not the first version of these books, as some of you may know. However, being an independent author comes with limitations, and for me at least, a great deal of impatience. When I wrote the original *Dark Corner* book, it was in the midst of the Coronavirus Pandemic, and the UK was in its first official lockdown. Go nowhere, do nothing, see nobody.

Basically my life in a nutshell, if you exclude going to work.

But I learned one day in my miserable and bland meandering through the days, that self-publishing had been on the rise while I looked the other way dreaming of having the time and money to be able to potentially have a crack at finally getting all of the stories out of my head. But better than that, was when I discovered there was a way to do it for FREE!

Note From The Author

I was warned by several forums and articles that KDP, although an excellent resource compared to the previous nothingness, was also full of issues, pitfalls, and Amazon's usual greedy ways. You will make no money, nobody will see your book if you have less than 50 reviews, and nobody reads horror these days anyway.

Sadly, I must admit, that I was tempted to chuck the briefly stirred ambition of mine in the bin, and carry on going to work everyday during an outbreak so people could buy their 'essential' bathroom paint or Sharpie marker pens.

But it was my wife who encouraged me to continue. She had always written both poetry and fan fictions, but had never felt comfortable with the idea of the world reading her work. She was, however, incredibly persuasive, and after I reworked a story I started writing 20 years previously into what became the first story, *The White Dress*, I got bit by the bug. Over the course of 2020, I wrote ten short stories varying in severity, but overall quite reserved for horror, and resolved to get them published come what may.

Sadly, I couldn't afford an editor or proofreader, and my wife was also working full time and so simply didn't have the time to read for me. And so I decided to publish through a previously unknown, to me at least, website called My Bestseller. They were based in the Netherlands, and required you to buy an ISBN number or publish without one. However, while they offered expanded distribution, this did not include Amazon. I also discovered after purchasing an ISBN for that original version of the book, that it came at a reduced cost for one reason. The code was registered to the website. Which meant exclusivity.

Bollocks.

Exclusivity and not even on Amazon? No this would simply not do. I did however, make it work for a while, and in the course of three months sold a whopping two copies. I bought more than that myself!

Then came the time to explore KDP properly. I had published the book on My Bestseller without ever proofreading or editing it. I figured nobody was going to read it so didn't really worry about it. But one day, when writing the stories for the second book, *Return to the Dark Corner*, I went back to examine plot points that could be expanded.

Shit.

Errors, grammar issues, typos everywhere and more worryingly, plot holes. But it wasn't too late! Barely anybody had read it so I could fix it! That's when I revised the book, and published through KDP, which came with free ISBNs! Jackpot I thought! But you must remember I was incredibly naïve and undereducated in this area. Exclusivity was a requirement again, but I didn't care. It was Amazon! Everyone uses Amazon! I even got suckered into Kindle Unlimited with the promise of more royalties. They really do know how to con you into things!

Anyway, since then, the *Dark Corner* series has grown and grown, even into producing several pieces of merchandise for the series such as posters and keyrings. The series concludes in the 13th book, a number I chose because I figured it fitting for something that began as a horror series primarily, although it became so much more!

And when the opportunity came along to work with Christian Francis to redesign, reformat and relaunch the series with a new uniform and polished look, I jumped at the chance. Christian put the shine to my stories that I had always hoped to achieve, and even redesigned the covers for me to give it a true 'series' look. I will be forever grateful for his generosity, hard work, and friendship, and am honored for these versions of my works to fall under the banner of Echo On Publishing.

So here we are, entering the *Dark Corner* once again. But I don't do things lightly. These are not simply redesigns of the exact

Note From The Author

same work. Oh no. My conscience wouldn't allow that! So every single book has an extra short story included to further expand this varied, fascinating and horrific universe. Consider it my gift of thanks to you all for sticking with me, encouraging me not to give up, and pushing me to do better.

As always, I encourage you to be kind, be healthy, and stay safe.

And thank you.

David W. Adams
28th November 2023

For the readers of Resurrection,

This is the follow up I probably should have given you years ago.

May you find comfort in these pages that the characters you loved were not left behind.

PROLOGUE

The galaxy had never been smaller.
Once a place of beauty, exploration, and wonder, now a place of violence, destruction and fear. Since humanity was restored to the universe ten years previously, everything had changed. The lies of the Decimator tale, the true nature of the remaining Saxons to create dominance in every quadrant. All of this had led to the greatest instability ever seen. The humans were not ready. The Resurrection technology had failed spectacularly, and the cloned humans and their recreated ancestors had become a plague rather than a victory. Their minds were scrambled, a blend of their memories and those they were derived from and infused with fractions of the lies they had been told. Hundreds of them had gone insane. Millions of lives had been lost as the swarm of mankind spread throughout the galaxy operating on fear and anger, determined not to face the same fate of extinction.

The screaming was now consuming the entire planet. People ran for cover, but the firing continued in incredible volumes. The green streaks from the ship's disruptors falling from the sky like rain, leaving nowhere to run. High above the surface, the large black vessels hovered, dominant in the golden skyline. As one of the vessels began to descend, it launched a torpedo from the rear launcher, striking the tallest remaining skyscraper at its core. The immense explosion blew right through the other side, the sound of creaking metal tore through the air, and as the building began to break in two, those hiding on the ground watched on as hundreds of people began leaping from the windows. The enhanced biological structuring of the Deltarians meant they were able to land from great heights with minimal damage, and many of them were able to sprint from the scene, but hundreds were just too high and perished as the building crashed down.

The dust cloud swept across the ground, gathering momentum until it finally dissipated. The engines from the Decimator vessels above glowed bright white, the light from them shimmering in the diamond skin of the victims lying below.

"Get these people to the evacuation ship NOW!"

As Fay'Lar ushered as many people from the shelter as possible, a landing party began running towards their location, indiscriminately firing at will cutting down men, women, and children in their path.

"D'Kar, get them to safety and I'll buy you some time!"

"You won't survive, Captain! You must come with us!"

Another barrage of firepower, and three Deltarian teenagers fell to the ground.

"Get out of here! That's an order Commander!"

D'Kar reluctantly nodded and turned towards the group and began ushering them forwards towards the location of their hidden ship. Fay'Lar removed her disruptor rifle from her back holster, checked the charge, and sprinted towards the oncoming forces.

She dived behind the remains of a school wall, the enemy firepower blasting chunks out of the stone. Leaning out to fire her own reply, her disruptor was hit, and the power cell blew. The minor explosion sent her flying backwards, and she was exposed without cover as they closed in. This was it. It was time for her to join her family once again. She closed her eyes and prepared herself for the final blow. But it never came.

A fast blanket of fire could be heard striking the approaching soldiers, and the sound of their bodies hitting the floor caused her to open her eyes. As she watched in disbelief, D'Kar sprinted past her, launching continuous fire with pinpoint accuracy. She had taught him well. Though they had been thrown together ten years before, they had grown incredibly close. She clambered to her feet and extracted her dagger from the left ankle holster. As her and D'Kar engaged in hand-to-hand combat, the two warriors began to persevere.

"I thought I told you to leave!" Fay'Lar screamed as she ran her blade through the chest of one of her attackers.

"I wasn't going to just leave you here!" D'Kar replied. "Besides, I'm a better fighter!"

The fact that she was able to laugh during a battle was one of the reasons her and her Commander were so close.

"Well, I did teach you everything you know!"

""Yeah, but I managed to repair most of that damage with real training!"

As the final human attacker was slain, the planet began to shudder violently.

"What the hell was that?" asked D'Kar.

They looked around for the source of the tremors but saw nothing. Another violent shake, and a small collection of buildings began to tumble. It was at that point that Fay'Lar saw what the humans were doing. The larger ship was firing a barrage of energy beams into one of the mining shafts in the distance.

"Oh my God."

Five torpedoes entered the shaft, and almost immediately, the surface began to shift, and huge cracks began shooting along the ground before the surface itself began to part.

"They're targeting the planet's core."

D'Kar grabbed Fay'Lar by the arm and pulled her away from the scene. They ran as fast as they could, leaping over the cracks as more and more appeared. Ahead of them, more ground troops were slaughtering their people. A sharp left in the market square and they re-joined the remaining few people entering the tunnel leading to the escape shuttles. As they entered, D'Kar turned to shut the barricade door, but spotted a child stuck under one of the fallen stalls. He glanced at Fay'Lar, and they exchanged a look. His said that he had to go help, but her eyes were pleading him to stay. But he'd made his decision.

Launching himself through the doorway back into the line of fire, he leapt over barrels of Salurian ale, and slid across the ground narrowly missing a falling lighting rig. As he reached the child, he could see her foot was broken. He fought against the tremors as he tried to lift the stall from her ankle, using all his might, but he couldn't quite shift it. It was at this point that D'Kar noticed the laceration in his right arm, the blood shining as much as his skin.

"Pretty sure I taught you how to bandage wounds too, Commander."

Fay'Lar had now appeared next to him and the two of them smiled at each other as they lifted the wreckage off the child. Fay'Lar picked the girl up and they once again sprinted back towards safety.

"I'm getting too old for all this running!"

D'Kar couldn't help but laugh at his Captain, knowing full well she was only four years older than him. But his smile was short lived as he saw a stone column begin to collapse right above the entrance to the tunnel. They weren't going to make it, and he had to decide. As they got within six feet of the entrance, and the stone fell from the sky, D'Kar launched his shoulder into Fay'Lar's back and her and the child were shoved through the entrance. As they tumbled into the tunnel, the column crashed down, destroying the entrance and crushing D'Kar beneath it.

The elders took the child and hurried towards the shuttles while Fay'Lar stared at the rubble now blocking the tunnel. She would mourn but now was not the time. The planet was becoming more and more unstable, and they had to leave. Her heart burned with rage as she tore through the caverns and entered the final shuttle. As the hatch was closed, the automation systems began the launch sequence. Rock was now cascading down from above as the planet began to break apart. The escape doors above opened, and through the windows, the passengers could see the Decimator vessels leaving and entering the upper atmosphere. The shuttle was not equipped with weaponry or high-speed engines, so Fay'Lar took over the controls.

Disengaging the auto pilot, she steered the ship in the opposite direction to the Decimators. As they began to climb, the Deltarian people looked down and watched as the surface began to collapse in on itself. The remaining buildings fell into the fiery abyss, and the parents shielded the eyes of their children. The shuttle emerged into space, and Fay'Lar pushed the engines to their maximum. As they reached the penal colony orbiting the first moon of Deltaria, the planet erupted, and the entire world blew apart. A shockwave emanated from the explosion and blew the prison structure apart like tissue paper, and despite their best efforts, the escape shuttle was caught in its wake. As the engines failed, and the vessel span out of control towards the surface of the second moon, on the other side of the shockwave, the Decimator ships exited the system.

1

"Bull shit."

"Excuse me?"

"I said it's bull shit! No way did that happen!"

"You're in the same universe that I'm in, aren't you?"

"Yes. But I'm beginning to think you may be in a world of your own entirely."

"Just because you've lived in a box in pieces for thirty years doesn't mean it didn't happen, Quincy."

"Okay, okay, let me get this straight."

"Go for it."

"A few hundred years ago, Earth was destroyed by The Decimators."

"Yes."

"But this Saxon guy saved one human?"

"Correct. Molly."

"And he was then attacked by some big Deltarian dude?"

"Lu'Thar. Yeah, he wanted the Resurrection technology."

"Of course, he did, who wouldn't?"

The sarcasm in Quincy's voice also made it slightly higher pitched. As he drank his drink and continued trying to swallow the facts, he carried on with his attempted story reconstruction.

"But the technology was actually an advanced cloning system which not only cloned this Molly chick a bunch, but allowed them to bring back copies of her ancestors from her DNA?"

"Pretty messed up right?"

"Yes, Jaxx. That's pretty messed up. So, then this chick is thawed out by mistake during an attack and is sent away with knowledge of how to fight and what was happening and had to make it on her own for a decade."

"Not quite. The real Molly was moved somewhere secret, and one of the clones was sent away with the skillset pre-loaded in her brain."

"Naturally. So, this clone thought she was the real deal and spent her years trying to find the Saxon dude and the technology and bring the humans back?"

"Yeah."

"But in the end, it turned out that the Saxons were lying, and the Decimators were really humans that they had previously cloned from kidnapped humans, who went insane and blew up their own planet?"

"Yup."

"And then just went to sleep on the far side of the galaxy for a couple hundred years?"

"Hey, blowing up a planet is hard work."

"Yeah, I can imagine. But then you met the clone chick, joined her on her adventure, and then the truth all came out in some explosive style and final confrontation with the Saxons, the clones and the Deltarians?"

"Yeah."

"And you killed the cloned Molly because she was beginning to go nuts too, and she was gonna unleash all these other clones which would have killed the real Molly?"

"Yeah, seemed a good idea at the time."

"But it didn't work, the real Molly flew away, a bunch of human clones and Molly clones escaped, along with the ship, the…"

"Shadow."

"Yeah the Shadow, and then another secret base hidden at the heart of Deltaria, which really must have pissed off their military, had another batch of the mad bastards, who then hatched, killed their Saxon creators, and then travelled across the galaxy wiping out any world or species that didn't bow to their whim, whilst also going quietly insane? Did I get all that right?"

Jaxx downed his glass of fire whiskey and placed it on the table with a light thud.

"Yeah, that's about it."

Quincy leaned forward on the table, his cobalt blue mechanical eyes whirring around as if they were buffering on a computer screen.

"And you brought me out of the box and put me back together why?"

Jaxx paused for a moment and looked through the metal bars to the sky outside. The stars were shimmering, and he could just make out the edge of a nearby nebula. Although he was not what you'd call an explorer, he knew this was a part of the cosmos he did not know. He shifted in his chair, and the metal restraints holding his feet together clunked against the wooden table.

"I built you because I thought I had a jackpot find, and a way to get to the humans. I figured you'd be some super intelligent, highly skilled *Data*."

"A what?"

"It's a late twentieth century TV sh… never mind. The point

is, all I got was a normal strength, blue eyed drunken robot, who managed to get us captured with nothing to eat or drink for two days other than fire whiskey!"

Quincy picked up the bottle in the centre of the table, the liquid glowing in the dim light, before pouring another shot, and knocking it back.

"And your god-damn circuits are gonna be fried if you drink more of that stuff! You don't even need to drink!"

"Art is imitation, my cross-bred friend."

"Let me ask you a question, Quincy. Do you know where we are?"

"No."

"Do you know who captured us?"

"No."

"And do you happen to know how to get out of here?"

Quincy briefly looked excited for a second before slinking back down, arms on the tattered wood of the table.

"No."

Jaxx put his head in his hands and rubbed his eyes. Suddenly, he heard movement outside their door, and as he looked up, he heard a lock turn in the key. As the tumblers clicked and moved in the mechanism, the door swung open, and a tall black figure was stood in the doorway.

Quincy squinted, his eyes trying to focus or zoom on their captor, but the fire whiskey had indeed inhibited his ocular implants and he could not make out any fine details. Jaxx, however, recognised the clothing the person was wearing.

"I'm pretty sure when I sold you that clothing, you were about a foot taller, Preet."

Quincy was surprised that Jaxx appeared to know the person, but less surprised when he happened to be wrong. As the person entered the room, the light from the candles on the wall

Chapter 1

illuminated their face, and Jaxx's cockiness faded instantly. This was not Preet, a man whom Jaxx had once been hired by. The mission had been to track down the garments on display here when they were stolen from his family's burial ground.

"You're not Preet."

The figure thrust his hand forwards and gripped Jaxx's neck tightly and gestured upwards with such strength that his feet were dangling in the air, rattling the chains. No mean feat to leave a seven-foot man dangling.

"No, Valkor. I am not the one you call Preet. Although I do like his clothes. My name is Wild Bill McGee. I'm the law in this town and you're trespassing with your weird lookin' friend here."

Even whilst swinging in the air, Jaxx could not help but be confused at the sound of a southern drawl. This man was clearly alien in origin, a species Jaxx had never come across, but he was speaking as if he had come from a spaghetti western. Jaxx had only seen a few westerns during his human research as an infant, but there was no mistaking it. This man really thought he was a Wild West Sheriff.

"Y'all are gonna be hung tomorrow at noon. Best say your prayers, boys. That's the last sunrise y'all ever gonna see."

The alien dropped Jaxx back to the floor, swung around and slammed the door behind him. The creature himself was almost indescribable in any other way but a giant crow. His face and skin were of a deep black colouring and his legs appeared significantly thinner than his arms. The face, such as it could be called, was constructed from a long beak-like nose, wide mouth and piercing yellow eyes. Had the man actually had feathers, you would have thought him a mutant bird. As the locks clicked back into place, Jaxx gathered his composure and returned to his seat.

"What the fuck was that?!" he choked through short breaths.

"Well, that poor deluded bastard believes he is in a western in the late 1800's on Earth, and we are in some kind of recreation of a matching town. At least that's what it looks like to me."

Jaxx's eyes bulged at the sudden usefulness of his companion. A signal Quincy interpreted as a thank you.

"You're welcome," he said.

"How did you suddenly become a narrator on the situation?"

"I noticed his costume, the gun in his holster, and I linked it to our surroundings, the way he spoke, and a very old movie in my database, called *Back to the Future Part III*. The rest was easy."

Jaxx downed another glass of fire whiskey.

"Great. Now all we need to do is break out of a loony bin, find our ship and hit the road."

Quincy nodded.

"We are quite lucky. In the movie, the villain likes to do his killing before breakfast."

Jaxx chuckled at both the absurdity of their situation but also at the straightness that Quincy was making pop culture references without realising. Hundreds of years may have passed but a good line is a good line.

"Well, partner. Guess we better mosey on out."

Quincy tilted his head slightly, ignoring the attempt at humour from his companion. His whirring eyes were focussed on the ceiling. Following the android's gaze, Jaxx's eyes moved across the wood until they met the same thing that was now fixating them both.

"What is that?" he asked.

"That, my friend, is a glitch in the mainframe."

Jaxx looked over his shoulder, now expressing a rather different look.

"Quincy, stop looking through your movie quotes database. Nobody likes a smartass."

"Apologies, but nevertheless that is indeed a glitch."

Chapter 1

In the corner of the room, in the ceiling above one of two small windows into the room, was a fluctuating pattern of light and misaligned imagery.

"A hologram?" Jaxx pondered.

"Exactly."

Jaxx shuffled along the floor, his ankles still bound in chains until he reached a small table near the right hand window.

"Give me a boost, Quincy."

"Dude, I really don't think you wanna try that in those restraints."

"I know what I'm doing," came his curt reply.

Quincy held up his hands in surrender, and bent down to lift up Jaxx onto the table. The same wood that furnished the entire room made up the construction of the table, but it was clearly either deliberately weathered or just plain damaged because it was beginning to buckle under the weight of the Valkor before he had even reached his full height.

"Dude, hold the thing steady!"

"I am holding it steady. You're standing on a piece of garbage."

Jaxx cautiously moved his hands up the wall, maintaining enough balance to move his hand towards the apparent malfunction. As he slid his fingers into the aperture, he received a massive jolt of electricity which surged down his entire body and created a massive flash before catapulting Jaxx through the air and across the room. Quincy ducked as his friend passed over him and crashed down through an empty chair situated on the opposite wall.

"I told you that wasn't a good idea."

"Thanks. I really needed your level of sympathy."

Jaxx looked across the floor, when he saw something confusing.

"Where are your shackles?" he said in disbelief.

Quincy looked down at his own feet, and then replied with the straightest face he could muster.

"I took them off."

"What do you mean you took them off?!" Jaxx shouted. "When?!"

Quincy shrugged his shoulders.

"About ten minutes after we sat down at the table."

"Are you fucking kidding me?! How?!"

Quincy, again straight faced, gave his reply.

"I am rather strong. I'm an android."

Jaxx went to get up but had a sharp pain shoot through his thigh. As he fell back down, he saw a six inch chunk of splintered wood protruding from his leg. However, before he could worry about pulling it out, the door burst open and five identical looking aliens flew in, guns drawn, and their spurs jingling as their heavy footsteps hit the woodwork. Two grabbed Jaxx, and two more were on Quincy.

"I guess you two fellas can't be trusted to behave in a civilised manner after all. How about separate beds?"

The sickening grin on Wild Bill's face turned Jaxx's stomach, and the pain in his leg overrode the confusion at the fact there were four other identical Wild Bill's in the room. As they were both dragged out of the cabin, the small glitch in the programme began to increase and spread down the wall.

Whatever this place was, it was falling apart. And fast.

2

"So let me get this straight… you're *not* going to tell me where your crew is?"

The woman shook her head, and grunted in the negative, her mouth obscured by a cloth gag. Her face had been beaten significantly. Her lip was swollen and split in two places, glowing dark red against the blue of her skin. Her hair was matted with blood, and her left eye swollen shut. A deep cut to her right eyebrow had sent more blood streaking down the side of her face where it dripped onto her shirt, below which was a small gunshot wound to her side. Both of her legs had been broken and there was bone protruding through the skin on the left leg. And despite all of this, she remained resilient and determined to keep quiet.

"You do realise that I will find out eventually? All you are doing is prolonging the inevitable."

Again, the woman remained quiet. And a further blow to the face was delivered by one of the other humans. Pulling her back up by her hair, a third human slammed her back down on the ground hard directly onto the protruding bone. Her screams felt like they could shatter the glass in the ship windows. Once she regained her breath, she noticed the blow had loosened her gag and she spat it free. An act which did not go unnoticed by the man in charge.

"Ah, finally. Do you have something to say to me, my dear?"

The woman summoned all her remaining strength, turned her head towards him, and gave what she suspected would be her final reply.

"I've only got one thing for you, Slater," she said.

"And what might that be?"

"Go fuck yourself."

Jack Slater's face did not change for a moment. The woman initially pleased with her parting shot, slowly lost her smile, but as she lost hers Slater gained his. He let out a wheezing chuckle before a full-blown belly laugh. As he calmed himself, he gestured to the two guards either side of her and they grabbed her arms tighter and lifted her to her feet. Another nod from Slater and they dragged her over to the nearest wall, slamming her back against the metal of the starship's interior. Slater wandered over to her, removing a short-handled blade from a pouch on his belt.

"Your people attacked my ships. They had the audacity to try and protect themselves from our invasion force. Had they simply handed over their weapons, we may have spared them. But they didn't. They destroyed two of my ships!"

The anger resonated along the walls, and visibly shook his own men momentarily. He calmed himself once more and continued until he was stood directly in front of the woman.

"You know, in the olden days, hunters on my world would take trophies from that which they hunted. Whether that be the antlers of a deer, or the head of a bear. They would mount them on a wall. Some cultures would carve the skin from their enemies, especially if their victim had distinctive body markers."

He looked down at the woman's chest and noted the top of

something visible on her dark blue skin just above the line of her blood-soaked shirt.

"Like tattoos."

He gripped the shirt in one hand, and ran the blade up through the middle, slicing the fabric from her body revealing a chest tattoo bearing the flag of her home world. Discarding the torn shirt to the ground, he plunged the blade into her chest and began slicing around the marker, blood oozing down her body, the woman screaming in pain and agony. As Slater removed the blade, and held the piece of skin in his hand, the woman's cries died down, her strength finally depleted. As she glanced up towards her abuser, Slater flashed the blade through the air, and ran the tip across her throat.

Dropping her body to the floor, one of the guards walked towards his Commander.

"Sir, if the rumours are true…"

"We do not have confirmation of that yet Mr. Halstone," Slater interrupted.

"But if they are?"

"Then we will stop them. This galaxy must remain in our grasp. If this fabled story of an uprising is true, we must make it our mission to quash it first. Mankind will not face destruction again."

Slater tucked the skin flap into a second pouch on his belt, which contained several others. He addressed his officer to set course for the nearest repair facility, before leaving the bridge area. As the door closed behind him, Slater collapsed to one knee, and gripped the sides of his head as severe pain tore through his body. Shooting pain going between both temples forced him to grit his teeth and close his eyes so tightly that the skin surrounding them went white. Flashes of words and distant memories bombarded his mind, and no matter how hard he tried, he could not make sense of any of it.

And then as quickly as the attack began, it stopped.

Slater looked down at his hands, which had balled into fists, and it was then that he realised they had been so tightly clenched, that his fingernails had pierced his palms. A thin trickle of blood emerged from each. He opened his hands, and used his right arm to ease himself up, balancing on the wall as he went. This was the second time in a matter of hours that this had happened. He glanced around but saw no crew, and so straightened his shirt and headed off down the corridor. After passing two security guards en-route, Slater reached a dark maroon coloured door marked 'EXECUTIVE OFFICERS ONLY'.

Once again, he checked to see he was alone, before typing in a security code on the panel to the right of the door. It slid open only enough for Slater to slip beyond the threshold, before closing behind him. The room was a stark contrast to the black and silver of the corridors with their maroon, red doorways. It was clinical white, the walls only penetrated by a thin blue strip light running the circumference of the rounded room. However, the unusual shape of the facility was not the main feature. In a matching circle, laid out before him was a circle of bio-beds. Every bed contained a body. A human body. The screens on the walls showed the readouts of each person and featured the time of their death, personal details and the symptoms that preceded their demise.

"Computer, call up the medical records of the most recently deceased member of the crew. Please recount symptoms leading up to their death."

A beep of acknowledgement echoed around the sterile environment, before the AI responded.

"*Officer 64532. Lieutenant Jason Grossman. Biological age 27.*

Chronological age 4 years old. Death occurred 72 hours ago. Symptoms prior to death included severe cerebral pain, hallucinations, anxiety, nausea, loss of memory and chronic fatigue. Death was caused by complete synaptic shutdown. Cause of synaptic degradation unknown."

Slater flinched at the sound of the symptoms matching his own. He read several records of other people, as he had done since the first person had died almost twelve months ago. All died from similar circumstances, and in relatively short time periods from the exposure to the first symptom. So far, he had lost ten crew members. The crew were only aware of the first three, who he managed to pass off as deaths in battle. But as he began to exhibit similar issues, he decided to keep the deaths quiet. Even his medical officer wasn't involved. His attempts to reclaim the information and records from either of the Resurrection chamber sites had failed due to the levels of destruction, and the remaining Saxons and the Shadow were still missing.

But right now, he had bigger problems to deal with. The people of this sector of the galaxy had been extremely resistant to the human domination and for the first time, the so-called Decimators were losing people and ships. Besides that, there was now talk that there were species willing to risk everything to reach what many people called the Unity – some kind of intergalactic alliance set against them. And that was a risk that the humans could not take.

"Captain Slater?" a voice came over the communications system.

"Slater here."

"Sir, we think we have a lead on the woman. Her ship was spotted in the Frankar System two days ago."

For the first time today, Slater felt like smiling genuinely and not part of a performance during an interrogation. He logged off the screens and walked towards the door.

"Excellent."

3

The rainstorm was now becoming more and more violent as the wind levels increased to their highest strength so far. The rocks high above the ground began to buckle under the combined pressure from the heavy striking water and the unrelenting force of the wind. Inside the cavern, the water level also continued to rise as the tide began to make its way in. This was not the best place to conclude a business deal. And yet it was the least likely place to be discovered. Especially the way the universe was right now.

Business deals were few and far between now that the humans had essentially taken over the galaxy. Entire worlds were being destroyed every month. Species were either being wiped out or enslaved and there seemed to be no way to stop them. The Deltarians were the latest to discover that incredibly definitive fact.

"This guy had better hurry up or we're gonna end up drowning never mind being caught!"

"Be quiet Saltair. It was your idea to strike this deal in the first place. Besides, our biggest worry was the Deltarian military, and they're all gone, so relax."

The man named Saltair was not your typically inconspicuous individual. Standing at eight feet tall, but incredibly slim in build, the damp air settled on his brown and speckled skin, shining like the skin of a snake. His eyes were a piercing deep blue and almost illuminated the area before him, such was their brightness. Hair similar length to that of a Saxon, the blonde twisted locks hung below the base of his spine, swaying as he moved.

Saltair was from a species known as The Others. Not much was known about their origins, other than they were a long-lived species who had resided on the edge of the galaxy in peace until the humans came back. Most had been dragged into service building the ever-increasing Decimator fleet and the rest had fled their space scrounging where they could and finding any work that would put food on their table. Some of the more unscrupulous members of the race such as Saltair, were prepared to do the dirtier side of the jobs on offer to keep themselves alive. As most people quickly guessed upon meeting Saltair, he had been a politician on his home world. And all these years later, he was still looking after number one at the expense of everyone else.

His companion, however, was the opposite. Krenik was no more than five feet tall, very much stockier than his friend, and completely bald. His eyes did not glow. They were completely black, along with his teeth and his skin was grey and mottled. Had he been a human, there would be grave concern for his health based on such an appearance. His race was well known. The Janko were an industrial people. They built anything and everything that they were asked. No race in the known universe could manufacture products, ships, weapons and construction resources faster or better than the Janko. It was due to this fact that they had escaped destruction thus far. They were the ones supplying the engines and weapons to the Decimator vessels. Krenik on the other hand, had chosen to go into business for himself. That was until he came

Chapter 3

across Saltair. Now he was more of a bounty hunter and junk collector. Something he often resented, but in truth he was making more money this way than as a franchisee, and so for now, was happy to continue. If it didn't get him killed.

"Well, Krenik, not everyone is closer to the ground than their dinner table. Aren't you due a growth spurt at some point?"

Krenik sneered at his companion, spittle flying through his pointed teeth and joining the now several feet of water they were standing in.

"At least I don't need to eat as much as you, you lanky piece of scum!"

"Watch your tone, midget, or I'll feed you to the whales of this planet. I hear they have a distinct taste for flesh."

Krenik reeled in his temper and did his best to calm down. He was still attempting to get the thought of flesh-eating whales out of his mind. Especially as with the ever-encroaching tide, the water they were standing in was getting deeper by the minute.

"How… how big are these whales? You know, the flesh-eating ones?"

Saltair chuckled. He often had disagreements with Krenik, but he admired his friend. It was easier to complete jobs with someone of his talents, and it was nice to have likeminded company.

"Do not fear, my friend. They need at least five feet of water to swim in. We're only up to about four and a half."

Krenik shot him a concerned look, and Saltair winked one of his blue eyes in jest. Although the sarcastic remark didn't seem to calm his associate.

As a crash of thunder echoed around the cavern, and the sky lit up with green lightning, the two men stumbled back at the sight of an illuminated silhouette. A cloaked person now stood in the entrance to the cave itself and although they were several metres away, Saltair and Krenik could see the glimmer of a sword at the persons' side. The lack of light kept most details to the shadows, but the cloak did appear to be not dissimilar in colour to the lightning which streaked the sky. A more blueish tint to the green. The blade, however, was clear to see. The design had a small hollow section two thirds of the way down the shaft of the blade itself. The design was unmistakable.

"Do you have what I asked for?" came the metallic echo of a simulated voice.

Krenik took several steps back behind his friend, as Saltair moved the opposite towards the figure.

"Do you have our payment?" he replied.

The mystery figure reached inside their cloak and pulled a small case free of the material, before tossing it towards Saltair who caught it in his tendril like fingers. Examining it in the light of his eyes, the item was satisfactory.

"And my request?" repeated the mechanical voice.

Saltair handed the small case to Krenik, who opened it up to reveal at least thirty rolls of golden coins before closing it back up and putting it into his own carry case.

"You know, this one was harder to catch than the others. She seemed quite insane. Almost cost me my ship. The price needs to go up."

The figure took another step forwards, and raised their sword to an elevated position, blade pointed at Saltair.

"The price was agreed. Give me the woman or this arrangement ends with your lives."

Saltair was not a pushover, but he was not a stupid man either. He knew sooner or later this arrangement would come to an end. They had delivered fifteen of this cargo so far, and there were only rumoured to be twenty total remaining.

"Very well, but I may need more time to find the next so we

can repair the damage. Krenik is good, but he is slowing down in his old age."

Saltair raised his arms in front of him and waved them across each other. As he did so, a cloaking field began to disengage to the left of the cavern entrance, and as it lowered, it revealed a cowering woman approximately thirty-five years of age, human with blood trailing down from her nose. Her eyes were darting in all directions, and she was mumbling words and fractured sentences to herself.

"*Decimator...lies...Torath...Saxon...saved...lies...chamber...broken...chamber...Shadow...gone...help me...*"

Saltair gestured towards the woman on the ground.

"See? Completely deranged. Her mind is broken. Hard to believe people clamoured for the technology that created her. I do wonder why you keep requesting the same cargo."

"That is not your concern."

"You know that Saxon blade of yours would fetch a hefty price in the Draylon System if you were tempted to part ways with..."

"Leave."

The two 'businessmen' didn't need to be told twice. They returned to each other's side, and Krenik tapped a panel on his belt. The two men teleported up through the cavern roof, leaving the woman and the stranger. As the wind howled ever harsher, the hood of the stranger blew down revealing that she too was a woman, long dark hair flowing from below the neckline of her helmet. She stood over the woman now sitting in the sea water up to her waist. She knelt in front of her and tapping a small circular button on the side of her neck, opened the helmet revealing her face and unmasking her voice.

"Look at me."

The stranger was now speaking to the woman softly. The woman continued to babble away.

"*Torath...resurrection...lies...decimators weren't real...humans...clones...Shadow...*"

The woman looked up, and her eyes bulged wide.

"*You...you...are...you...are......me!*"

"No," said Molly, her cloak whipping up behind her. "You are me."

As she pulled back her sword, the moonlight glinted on the steel blade. With one swift thrust, she drove the blade straight through the heart of the cowering clone and as she did so, closed her eyes tightly, clenching to keep her tears in. She held the clone tightly in her free arm as she listened to the life leaving her.

"Now your mind is at peace. You can rest."

Molly pulled the sword free, and the clone slumped to the floor. She stood up and slid her blade into a holster on her back. Pulling her hood back over her head from where it had slipped, she pulled a small capsule from her pocket, and tossed it onto the body of the woman lying in the sea water. As Molly exited the cave back into the harsh weather, the capsule dissolved, and a thin glowing mesh of orange enveloped the body briefly before vanishing. As the glow left, the clone body turned to ash, and drifted away in the winds of the storm.

With one command to her wrist communication device, Molly dematerialised in a shimmer of light which then shot upwards towards the heavens. Seconds later, she appeared on the teleportation pad onboard a rather derelict vessel. Water dripped from corroding pipes above her, and the clunking of loose metal deck plating echoed around her as she walked towards the cockpit.

"Welcome home," a deep female voice offered.

As she span around in the seat, Molly was greeted by a familiar diamond skinned smile.

"Did you get what you needed?" she asked.

Molly slumped down in the seat next to her.

Chapter 3

"Another one off the list," replied Molly.

"Isn't it about time you told me what's going on?" the Deltarian female asked. "Or do you still not trust me?"

She walked across the enclosed space to a small table towards the back wall which contained two shot glasses and several bottles of liquid, each more colourful than the last. Molly got up and moved to join her.

"It's not that I don't trust you, Narlia. It's just that I… don't trust you."

"You do realise that's complete bullshit, right?"

Molly laughed as she reached for a bottle nearby. Pouring her and Narlia a glass of the dark blue liquid, she downed the entire contents in one fell swoop, before again reaching for the bottle of Beresian brandy and pouring herself another large measure.

"Look, if you really want me to trust you, then you must understand that I am truly not like them. Hell, I wasn't even around when these bastards were created."

Narlia downed her own drink, as the ship gave a harsh rattle. She stood up and walked back to the console to check the ship was still on course for their destination. Everything seemed fine.

"Stupid rusting piece of shit." She paused. "You didn't know my father, did you? That was… the other you."

Molly shook her head.

"Then all you've seen of him, is what you've read in reports and Deltarian military files and hear say."

Molly poured Narlia another drink and stood up to join her at the command console. She handed her the drink and sat in her chair.

"So, tell me about him. What happened to you? You've not told me much of anything since I picked you up floating in that escape pod. It's been four months. Have I ever given you any reason not to trust me?"

Narlia waited a moment before her response in the form of another question.

"No. You haven't. But by the same token, have I ever given you reason not to trust me?"

Molly shook her head.

"No. You haven't. In fact, if it wasn't for you, I'd probably have been blown out of the airlock when we raided the *Shadow*."

"Exactly. Especially given the fact there was nothing on it but squatting mercenaries. Another waste of time to add to our ever-growing list of failures."

"Narlia?"

Narlia sighed, and sat down opposite her new friend, sipped from the new drink, and took a deep breath.

"My father was a dictator. He knew what he wanted, his path was always going to be in the military, and nothing was going to get in his way. For a while, he changed. He became this amazing person to be around, and I genuinely thought, even at such a young age that there may be a better life than staying on a desert rock hollowing out our own planet."

Molly squinted for a moment as she realised what she was referring to.

"When he met Torath?"

Narlia nodded.

"Torath was on a mission to rescue endangered species, save creatures on the brink of extinction. It was a worthy cause. Then when Dad asked him to help save Deltaria and he refused, he knew something must be wrong. Then he investigated Torath's dealings, and he realised he was dealing with Kaleys and other mercenaries and pirates. Saxons would never do that. That's when he turned on Torath. And returned to his old ways. He became a wrecking ball, swinging through the galaxy, crushing anyone that got in his way."

"How old were you?"

Chapter 3

Narlia gave a sarcastic chuckle.

"I was four years old. He claimed that I was the most important thing in his life, but all I did was get shoved to the back of whatever ship he was on, or whatever conference room he was in. He didn't even notice when my mother died. She was killed in a home invasion by some protesters who figured they could get the military to stop mining if they hit the family of the head of the operations. It took six days for him to respond to the communication that she was gone, and I was alone."

Molly had no words to offer her. She had experienced distanced relationships with her mother being in the military. And her father had always seemed lost after it had happened. That's why she joined the military herself, to try and get closer to her mother in the hopes that her father would reconnect with her. She noticed tears forming in Narlia's eyes, so she handed her the bottle of brandy. Narlia chuckled and accepted it.

"He received word that a new vein of Serenite had been found in one of the caverns in the main shaft. Now this was a material which had been mythical up to that point, and nobody knew how it got there. So naturally, he led an away mission to explore it. He told me that it was no place for a child, and I was to stay behind alone. But all I wanted was to be with my father. He was all I had. So, I snuck onto the ship, and hid in the cargo bay. As I started to climb out of the container I'd hidden in, the ship was struck by falling rocks, and the engines damaged. I heard the call for the crew to abandon ship, and by the time I fought my way to the bridge, the ship was falling into the darkness, and I watched my father's escape pod shoot up into the sky."

Molly's eyes were wide with intrigue and disbelief. She had seen some pretty horrible things in the last ten years, but this was heart-breaking.

"How did you survive?" she asked, almost pleading for a happy ending, even though she knew there wasn't one.

"Deltarian mining ships are tough. When the ship was buried, most of the bridge stayed intact. I managed to get some emergency rations out of one of the medical consoles near the tactical station. After three days, I was asleep, running out of air, and I felt the ship move. I mean it was moving downwards."

"But I thought you were buried on the bottom of the shaft?" asked Molly, now fully confused but invested.

"I was. The debris began to shift, and after what felt like thirty minutes, the ship jolted to a halt, and the bridge doors were forced open. And that's when I met Reyton."

Molly's face took a sour turn.

"Reyton. Don't talk to me about that prick."

Narlia nodded.

"How much did he tell you? You know, before you blew up his ship?"

The two of them laughed, despite the violent nature of the statement.

"Something about trying to preserve humanity and dozens of other species, but there would need to be sacrifices, blah blah blah."

Narlia laughed again.

"Yeah. He told me my father was still alive, and that humans were responsible for attacking Deltaria, and they were holding him hostage. Then, when I escaped and saw that they were cloning the humans, he switched his story to something along the lines of humans created the clones and they had defects, so they were trying to rescue the new clones, and I must stay tucked away and await my father's triumphant return."

Molly raised her eyebrows.

Chapter 3

"Why was he so intent on keeping you there? I mean what purpose could a Deltarian kid serve?"

Narlia shrugged her shoulders.

"I don't know. Never found out. I was too fixated on the slim chance my father was still alive."

"But you knew he was dead?"

"I suspected. I heard murmurs, and suggestions that this facility had been recently activated by some sort of emergency protocol. But I waited. Trying to figure out how to get out of there. Eventually, I was gifted one."

"Slater."

Narlia nodded.

"Yup. Reyton released the human clones, and they turned. The defects remained, and they killed everyone in the facility. Except Reyton. That cowardly bastard managed to escape. Once the humans had gone, I made my way to one of the remaining escape pods and went looking for my father and clues about what had happened."

Molly held her glass up towards making a toast.

"And then we met!"

Narlia laughed.

"Well, there were about nine and a half years in there somewhere, but yeah then we met. How about you?"

Molly stood up and walked towards the back of the cockpit, pacing slowly and glancing down at the sword she had taken from the Saxon ship she left the Resurrection facility in.

"By the time I got to Deltaria, there was nothing left of the facility, and the military wouldn't help me. As far as they were concerned, I was the lone human woman who killed dozens of their operatives, their head of the military, destroyed their flagship, and helped build the resurrection tech."

"But that wasn't you," Narlia offered.

"I knew that, but they didn't care. Their planet was in chaos. I didn't know where I was, who I was or any significant information. All I knew was what was in the ship's logs that Torath had left behind. I knew they were mostly lies, but it was all I had to go on."

Narlia's tone shifted before posing the next question.

"Did they torture you?"

There was silence for what seemed like an eternity, before Molly turned her head back towards her slightly, and gave a gentle slanted nod.

"They thought I had information about what happened in the nebula. They broke my jaw, my nose, my ribs. Even fractured my left scapes. It's one of the bones in the ear."

Narlia held up a hand as if to say, 'please don't patronise me.' Molly held up a hand in apology and moved on.

"When the Allurians came and launched an attack on the penal colony, they took me as a hostage. Kept me locked in a room on their ship, until we reached a trade station in the Nervala System. They traded me to a Kaley Captain for a supply of engineering parts. I knew if I didn't act, I'd be traded for the rest of my life. So, I did what I had to do."

"He was your first kill?"

Molly nodded, clearly disturbed by what she had done even after ten years.

"He tried to 'rent' me out as entertainment. The first night he tried it, I ran a sharpened piece of wood through his heart and ran for the nearest airlock. Thank God for automated ships... and *Star Trek*."

Narlia was confused.

"*Star Trek?*"

Molly chuckled to herself.

"It's an old Earth science fiction series. The computers on their starships were voice activated. It's what made me think to try it when I escaped."

"You mean like historical documents?" Narlia asked.

"Are you serious?" she asked in reply.

Narlia was confused and said nothing in reply. Molly chuckled again.

"Okay, sit down there, *Galaxy Quest*. I found out that the other clones of me from the facility and from the *Shadow* were still out there, but their minds were degrading. One showed up on Dera Prime and interrupted a deal I was trying to put together to repair my engines about a year and a half after my escape. There were reports all over the sector of humans showing up confused, in pain, and ripping themselves apart. And that's when I made it my mission to find them and put them out of their misery."

Both women let out an elongated sigh. Now they were both mostly up to date. But one thing did occur to Narlia.

"But what about the guy you told me about? Drax? Shax?"

"Jaxx."

"Yeah, the orange dude. Didn't he kill your clone, or duplicate or whatever she was? I mean he's a bad guy too right?"

Molly thought long and hard for a moment. It was a long time since she had seen Jaxx run his blade through her clone. It was the one other loose end she hadn't felt like she had tied up. She gestured at her Saxon blade.

"Let's just say if I ever run in to him, I'll have a big decision to make."

4

The high pitched screech jolted Fay'Lar awake and she sat bolt upright and drew her blade staring into the darkness that surrounded her. Again the scream, but seemingly further away. Her eyes darted left to right but she saw nothing. Then silence. The sound of her own breathing filled the room and she could hear her blood pounding in her ears. And then footsteps. Heavy and metallic in sound. The clunking of boots on a deck. She must be on a ship of some sort. But it certainly wasn't where she had been after the crash.

The footsteps seemed to reach her location before stopping, and again for a moment or two there was silence. Suddenly a rectangular shaft of light burst through the darkness as a hatch was slid open, and the light sent Fay'Lar cowering back for the darkness. Squinting she attempted to focus. She could make out two dark red eyes staring back at her but nothing more. The hatch was slid closed and then the door was yanked open. The red eyes and the body which they belonged to entered the room, blocking out much of the doorway and the light.

"You, female. Get up."

Still struggling to see, Fay'Lar responded weakly.

"Wh-wha-what?"

Angered by her lack of response, the man charged forward, baring his teeth. As he reached down to grab her by the arm, Fay'Lar threw her arm forwards and plunged her blade into the right side of his neck. All of her strength went into the attack, and as he screamed out in pain, and began to choke on his own blood, she pushed him away and struggled across the floor towards the door. But the assault had attracted security and before she reached the opening, five Allurians surrounded her and began kicking her in the ribs until she stopped moving. Two Allurian officers knelt down and each grabbed an arm, lifting her limp body from the floor before carrying her along a corridor.

Barely conscious, she could make out the familiar layout of an Allurian warship. But something here was different. The soldiers seemed on edge. Almost panicked over something. She thought she heard the word 'human' uttered, but her mind was battered and she couldn't truly think straight. The remaining strength in her legs left her and she allowed her feet to drag on the metal deck, and felt herself being swung around a corner before entering another room. The two Allurians holding her lifted her high into the air, and slammed her down onto a nearby bed, before strapping her down.

Even as tough and as much of a warrior as she was, Fay'Lar simply did not have the energy or body strength to fight against the restraints.

She heard the guards leaving the room before the air was pierced by the sound of a whistle. The tune sounded familiar but distant. The more she tried to decipher the melody, the closer it became, until in front of her was another Deltarian, whistling the tune from her favourite lullaby as a child. Her eyes bulged in fury that a noble Deltarian could be working with the Allurians, but she did not have the physical protest available to match it.

"I believe you know that little tune, my dear."

Fay'Lar did not respond, and instead gritted her teeth.

"That's alright, you don't have to answer me. Every child on our home world knew that song. It was my daughter's favourite."

Again, Fay'Lar remained silent, although it was becoming harder to do so.

"Captain Fay'Lar, I need you to tell me something, and I want you to know that one way or another I will extract the responses I need."

"And just what might that be?" she finally replied.

The man smiled at finally getting a response.

"I want you to tell me where Slater and his forces are going."

"How the hell should I know? I didn't exactly invite him to Deltaria!" she spat.

"Ah, but you did my dear."

Confused and shocked, the man stood aside and revealed a large computer monitor. As Fay'Lar managed to focus her attention on the screen, video footage appeared on it. She gasped in shock. She was looking at a still video image of her standing on the bridge of the *Challenger* talking to Jack Slater.

"But…but that…that never happened! That ship was destroyed nearly a decade ago!"

The man switched off the video, and walked around the bed until he was standing level with Fay'Lar's face.

"Now I know this video is a fake. But the soldiers on this ship are convinced that you attempted to lure the humans to the Allurian homeworld in an effort to spare your own planet."

As he was speaking this sentence in a more hushed way, Fay'Lar began to think something was not quite as it seemed. The man's eyes were almost pleading with her, not so much for information on a fraudulent video, but for help.

"But they destroyed Deltaria. They massacred our people. I don't understand."

The man now spoke loudly enough so the guards outside could hear him, but he did not change his facial expression.

"Because your plan backfired! The humans decided to target your planet first before moving on. And do you know why they think this? Why they are so full of rage and anger?"

Fay'Lar shook her head, and the man looked around before leaning in towards her ear.

"Because they're clones too."

He moved away and the begging in his eyes became more intense. Fay'Lar felt the pit of her stomach swirling. Surely this must be a ruse of some sort. The Resurrection technology was never used or stolen to her knowledge by anyone other than the Saxons and the humans themselves. While she was trying to contemplate this information, the man looked around again to ensure he wasn't being watched.

"My name is Vaysa. I was a chief medical officer on Deltaria for the military. When Lu'Thar left onboard the *Challenger*, I was his original choice of practitioner, but at the last minute there was an emergency at the University and the ship left without me."

A grumble by the doorway broke his speech. As he checked again, he found the coast clear to continue.

"I was then assigned to a vessel called the *Marlene* and on our first mission we came across this vessel. She was floating, powerless through space. The usual communications channels were inoperative so we boarded the vessel. We found over two hundred stasis pods, each containing an Allurian body. They had vital signs but they were in stasis. The curious thing was that they appeared to be on a timer. Thinking the timer was some kind of self destruct,

Chapter 4

our Captain ordered us back and we moved away to destroy the vessel. But the crew had awakened by this point, and pre-programmed with their knowledge and skills, they opened fire. They destroyed my ship, and captured my escape pod. Unsure about their condition, they kept me to act as their doctor. I have been trapped here for almost eight years, slowly watching the crew go insane. Somewhere in this Resurrection formula or code or whatever it is, there is a distinct flaw."

Vaysa reached down and injected a needle between two of Fay'Lar's scales and pushed a blue fluid into her body. Immediately she began to feel a surge of adrenaline, and could almost smile with the sensation now tearing through her body as she began to gather strength.

"Whatever it is, it causes paranoia first. Then come the bouts of anger, and rage, before eventually the mind tears itself apart. That video was created by me when I heard you were onboard. I needed to get them to bring you to me to help me."

Fay'Lar felt her restraints being undone, and in turn, she sat up and slid to the side now upright on the bed.

"What the hell did you give me, doc?" she asked, still slightly amazed at her recovery.

"A little something I've been working on. It boosts your system by over a hundred percent in every area. Mental acuity, physical strength, and stamina. But it only lasts for about fifteen minutes, so we don't have time to waste."

"How did you know who I am?" she asked.

"I worked with your father before he left Deltaria. When your parents were killed, I assumed you dead too, but when I found out you were picked up on that moon, I began to hope again. You were a strong willed child, and a keen athlete Fay'Lar. I have seen your military record and I knew you were the one to finally help me off this ship!"

"Where did the Allurians get this technology?" she asked, as she leapt down off the bed.

This alerted the guards who then charged into the room.

"Maybe a conversation for later!" Vaysa exclaimed as he dived to the side to avoid the swinging arc of an Allurian fist.

Fay'Lar ducked to miss the blow, before swinging around behind her attacker, and slamming her own fist into the base of his spine. Despite his heavy stature, the increased strength seemed to be effective, as he crumpled to the floor. She reached forward grabbing his head in both hands, and twisted it sharply to the left and up. The crack was audible around the room.

Dropping the first body to the floor, she rolled out of the way of the disruptor blast from the second Allurian, grabbing a sharp scalpel blade from a nearby instrument tray. The soldier continued to fire as he advanced on her position, but as he closed in, she dived underneath the bed she had previously occupied, rolled onto her back and ran the blade across the back of his foot just above the top of his boot. He screamed in pain and as he fell back onto the floor level with her, she plunged the blade directly into his throat. Both Fay'Lar and Vaysa were astonished at the effect of this serum, but already she could feel its effects diminishing.

"We need to hurry," she advised.

Vaysa nodded in agreement, and they left the infirmary and headed down the corridor.

"Are there others here?" she asked as they moved as quickly as they could.

"There were forty three of you brought on board. The Allurians murdered sixteen before they brought you to me. The others are being held in the aft cargo hold."

The stomach swirling began again. Twenty-seven. Is that all that were left of the Deltarian race? Surely there must be others out here. Twenty-seven. At last census there had been six-and-a-half-billion.

"Then that's where we are going!"

Vaysa followed her lead. She had boarded several vessels such as this in the past so she knew her surroundings. The only problem was the shuttle bay was in the opposite direction. A fact Vaysa appeared to be trying to bring to her attention.

"Don't worry about that, Doc. We aren't leaving this ship. The Allurians are."

5

"Okay you need to tell me about this stuff. If we are going to try and get there before everyone else, I think I deserve to know what I'm getting myself into."

Narlia was now sat at the same small table she had been at for the last two hours, watching as Molly scrolled through terraquads of information relating to the Unity. Her eyes had never left the screens, and Narlia could see her friend's mind absorbing the data like a sponge. She had heard rumours about this fabled place, this mystical organisation of species that were resolute against humanity, but had never seen any definitive proof that it even existed let alone what was there. Molly closed the screen down and span her chair to face her Deltarian companion.

"The humans under Slater have destroyed the galaxy as we know it. You've seen the destruction and the violence. The technology is appearing to be spreading through remaining cultures desperate to stop themselves from being annihilated. Everyone wants to resurrect their race before they die out completely. I even heard some Allurian war-lord had got their hands on a replica bootlegged version."

Molly glanced down at the floor as she thought about all the chaos that had come forth from the attempted resurrection of just one race. There was only one way the universe was heading.

"But for hundreds of years there have been rumours. What are the Unity? Are they a small group, a confederation of planets? Is it a place or a people? I found mentions of them in old ship logs even before Earth was wiped out. With humanity sweeping across not only our galaxy but the neighbouring ones, every species wants a way out. They can't defeat the Decimators, so they're trying to find this Unity."

Narlia shook her head.

"Yeah, yeah but all that is just a story. Does anyone actually know if they exist, or whether it's just an idea?"

Molly tapped a few commands into her console and brought the screen back up.

"Nobody can find definitive answers, but Reyton and his crew believed they had empirical evidence of its existence. Here, there is a report of radio transmissions coming from an asteroid belt, but no translation. Another report was from a Berzite vessel which reported seeing a giant structure on the surface of a previously abandoned moon. But if they are out there, we need to find them and soon."

Narlia raised her eyebrows in both disbelief and a sarcastic nature. It was a skill Molly had often found amusing, but in this case she felt like she was being called a liar.

"Okay, so there's this wonderous utopia where a group of space heroes are waiting to lead us all against humanity. Sounds like something from one of your old Earth shows to me."

Molly took a deep breath, trying to resist the urge to point out that was exactly what it was.

Chapter 5

"Hope. The belief that this united group of people can defeat the humans. In the last ten years, Slater and his crews have decimated over four hundred billion people. Four. Hundred. Billion. That kind of massacre drives the survivors to whatever measures they can cling on to. I've seen it in wars on Earth. When the hope is all you have, then you grab hold of it with all your might and you don't let go."

Narlia understood to a lesser degree. She had had similar hope when she believed her father was still alive. She remembered the day she found out he was dead. For a time, it felt like she had died too. But as she pondered that thought, she noticed Molly was looking at a different report in the data that she hadn't mentioned.

"So what do *you* believe?" she asked.

"What?"

"You clearly don't believe any of this. It's clearly bordering on religion to believe in a mythical people that can save the universe. So what do *you* believe?"

Molly re-read the report she had now perused what must have been fifty times by now. Rather than directly answer Narlia's question, she read the report out loud.

"An independent freighter captain reported reaching what he believed to be the Unity headquarters. When questioned further, he believed he was looking into some kind of galactic mission base. His ship was hidden in orbit, but at least three hundred were docked around the structure. However, when he returned just a day later, the base was gone. The captain's claims were dismissed as nonsense by the Deltarian militia tasked with his debriefing, due to the lack of evidence, questionable mental state and the fact that his flight recorder could not confirm the location in question."

This captured Narlia's attention slightly more than the other suggestions.

"Three hundred ships?"

Molly nodded.

"The captain of that freighter said he dropped a location beacon before turning back from fear of being caught, but no other ship has documented encountering it. But it did get me thinking. Maybe there is a space station out there where there are people massing to stop Slater. I managed to get hold of the supposed co-ordinates of this station. That's where we are heading next."

Narlia walked over to her friend, and placed a hand on her shoulder. Molly placed her own hand on top, and looked at her companion. There weren't many people that she could rely on, or trust. And despite a decade of fighting her way through a galaxy of things she still didn't fully understand, Narlia was the first person she had come to feel as a true friend. For that, she would always be in her debt.

"But in order to find out, we need to get there. And it's not a short trip."

Narlia sat beside her.

"How long?" she asked, fearful of the answer.

"For us to reach this location, we have to cross six star systems."

"Shit."

Molly nodded.

"Yeah. At maximum speed for this rig, we'd be looking at eight weeks."

Narlia tried to process this information.

"Sure gonna be a slow ride. Not to mention a drain on our limited resources."

Then she remembered the reason Molly had chosen to acquire this vessel in particular when they first met.

"Stasis pods."

"Stasis pods."

Chapter 5

Molly strolled past Narlia and left the cockpit, rounding the corner of the doorway into a small corridor. Narlia followed behind, and moments later they were standing in the entrance to the small cargo bay. Activating the lights, the room was illuminated and showed a row of six stasis pods lined up on the far wall.

"You took these from the *Shadow* didn't you?" Narlia asked.

Molly nodded.

When she had come across the derelict *Shadow* two years previously before she had met Narlia, Molly salvaged six of the pods that she herself had once been contained in. She'd heard the rumours of the Unity, and something told her she would need them.

"I was clinging to that same hope, even back then," she said. "We all long for a peaceful universe. Sometimes hope is all you have left."

Molly shut off the lights, and allowed the door to close before heading back to the cockpit with Narlia. As they sat back down at the console, Narlia didn't wish to press further, but the reality was they were taking a huge risk being only one of a number of interested parties. They'd be shot down or boarded in a mere matter of days if any attacker knew they were in stasis.

"You know we can't do this alone," she said. "There's no way we can float in space for eight weeks free of attack."

Molly nodded. She had already thought about that.

"That's why we are heading to a pit stop, if you like."

Narlia was confused.

"What kind of pit-stop?"

As if on queue, directly in front of them, two Allurian vessels dropped out of high speed, flanking their ship.

"What the hell?" proclaimed Narlia.

"Relax, they're here to talk."

47

Narlia reached behind her for her disruptor, and slid a thin blade into the top of her boot.

"Allurians don't talk, they shoot first and ask questions later!"

Molly smiled.

"These aren't what you would call standard Allurians."

"What are you talking about?" Narlia pressed with a sense of urgency.

A beeping noise came from the communications console alerting them to an incoming message. Molly reached across and opened the channel, and the face that appeared on screen gave her a much more relaxed feeling than she expected.

"Glad to see you made it, Fay'Lar."

Narlia's face was frozen. She was looking at not only another Deltarian face, standing on an Allurian bridge, but she was looking at her father's closest aid. Syl'Va had always been by Lu'Thar's side, but Fay'Lar was the hardest working, the one who spent more time around her and her family. Finally she felt that her connection with her father had been restored.

"Well I had a little trouble with the Allurian clones, but the doc here thinks he has managed to stabilise their condition, albeit temporarily."

Molly smiled.

"Nice to see you're both getting along now."

Fay'Lar rolled her eyes.

"A marriage of convenience, I can assure you."

She then switched gears.

"Have you had any luck locating Jaxx?"

Narlia snapped out of her frozen state. Jaxx? As in the tall muscular orange guy who stabbed her clone through the back? Detecting Narlia's eyes on her back, Molly changed the direction.

"Not yet, but I'm still looking. Have you heard from the Allurian Council yet?"

Chapter 5

Fay'Lar sighed deeply.

"The first communication we sent went unheard. The second one was met with the arrival of an Allurian Destroyer tasked with bringing us all in to custody. They didn't take too kindly when the third message we sent involved details of us blowing that ship out of the sky. I don't know if we can get them on board, Molly."

This time it was Molly who took a deep breath before sighing.

"We have to try. If we can find a few others, maybe we can convince them together. But we need to be quick. Slater's ships can't be that far away. He must have heard the same rumours by now."

Almost as the words left her lips, their ship rocked violently from weapons fire, as did the image on screen. Both ships had been hit and a quick glance out the window revealed the source.

"Slater."

"I guess we should press pause on this conversation for a moment. Excuse me while I kill him."

With that, Fay'Lar closed the channel, and her ship immediately launched towards the Decimator vessels. Molly couldn't help but smile. She hadn't had an abundance of contact with Fay'Lar since the destruction of the Resurrection facility, but it was good to see her fight remained strong. They had met properly when Molly managed to trade her way into a Deltarian school to pick up some valuable engineering lessons. Fay'Lar had been tasked with giving an emotional speech about loyalty and perseverance. Their paths had crossed a few times since then, but they had always kept contact.

As another hit jolted the ship, Molly turned to Narlia and gestured her to the weapons console.

"Time to go to work."

6

Despite the precarious position he found himself in, Jaxx could not help but stifle a snigger. Even Quincy was struggling not to laugh at loud. The sight was certainly an impressively absurd one. Whoever had designed this holographic simulation had clearly not intended to capture the pair, and certainly not intended to dispatch them. That much was clear.

The gallows with which both were to be hanged, stood only six feet tall from top to the hard wooden deck below. Jaxx was seven foot-plus and Quincy, apart from being an android and incapable of being hung, was at least seven feet tall. The spectacle now playing out in front of them both was of a group of crow-like aliens attempting to find a way to make the gallows taller. It was at this point that Jaxx noticed these creatures were also holograms, because as they started to interact with one another, their hands would merge or pass through another hand.

"Psst."

Quincy took his eyes off the debacle unfurling between them, and looked toward Jaxx who was trying to catch his attention.

"Yes?" came his simple reply.

"How about you use some of that secret strength you have to, oh I dunno, break free and rescue us?"

Quincy smiled and with one flick of an ankle, the braces holding his feet together snapped open. The crow-creatures were too busy fumbling to notice. But it was Jaxx who noticed something unnatural, just behind the gallows itself. He saw a small hut, no more than a couple of feet wide, with the door propped slightly ajar, and a glowing light coming from inside. He nodded his head towards it, and Quincy followed his gaze. He nodded in return, and with lightning speed that even Jaxx was not aware of, he broke free of his stocks, leapt off the stage, and ripped the door of the hut clean off its hinges.

Inside, a man screamed in a rather loud and particularly shrill manner. His arm quickly punched a few commands into a computer terminal situated in front of him, and the crow people dissolved.

"Ah shit, wrong button!"

Quincy reached down and grabbed the man by the scruff of the neck. He lifted him clear of the hut with one hand, and moved across to Jaxx, who had now leapt from the stage to the ground, and broke his friend free of his own restraints.

"You're human?" Jaxx asked, slightly alarmed.

"No I most certainly am not!" the man protested.

Whilst he did indeed look very much like a human, it was only upon close inspection that Jaxx noted a slight difference in skin texture around the neck and eye sockets. It was almost like a tattoo, but under the skin, rough to the touch and slightly darker than the natural skin tone.

"Is there any particular reason you were trying to make a Wild West killing machine to execute us in? I really would love to know."

Chapter 6

Quincy's unique ability to create sarcasm, wit and humour really did put him apart from any other artificial lifeform Jaxx had seen. But he did have a point.

"I'd answer him if I was you Mr Non-Human. I mean you did see what he just did to your restraints. Imagine if that were your neck."

Jaxx made a gagging noise for added effect, and the man's face changed from anger to fear.

"No, please, you mustn't. You weren't supposed to find us yet. We aren't ready. This was a testing ground. You wandered in by mistake. You're early!"

Now Jaxx and Quincy looked confused. Wandered into what? What was it they were early for? The man who was still dangling from Quincy's grip seemed to pick up on the confusion, and offered to clarify if Quincy put him down. Jaxx nodded approval, and the man once again found his feet on solid ground.

"This is Outpost 47. You're on a small testing site that we have been using to simulate battle scenarios for when the humans come. This one was designed to disorientate them, and confuse them in the hopes their in built malfunctions would accelerate."

For the first time in many years, Jaxx felt a complete seriousness. His mind clicked, and he remembered all of the rumours he had once heard amongst the other Valkor in his youth. Quincy clearly wasn't aware, having spent the last three decades in a box, but Jaxx knew where he was. He understood.

"This is the Unity."

The man nodded at him, his wispy hair falling into his face. He moved back toward the control panel in the small hut, and pressed a few commands. The entire simulation vanished. The saloon, the shack they had been held in, the gallows, even the dirt they'd been stood on. Now they found themselves stood on golden coloured rock in a small clearing in what looked like a desert. But it was what hung above them in the sky that Jaxx and Quincy were captivated by.

"No… fucking… way."

Quincy had never heard Jaxx use such profanity before, and despite the gravitas of the situation, he could not help but smile at his friend.

"That is indeed impressive."

Orbiting the moon they were stood on, was a gargantuan space station, rotating as if in its own orbit. The size of the thing was so vast, that not all of it could be seen at once. Jaxx counted at least twenty docking ports, and could see people walking around inside, even from this distance. The volume of ships was simply too many for him to process, and all of different designs.

"How many ships is that? I couldn't possibly identify all of those."

"Three-hundred-fifty-two."

Jaxx glanced over at Quincy and smiled.

"Well, you did ask."

The man pointed up at the various vessels.

"We started with sixteen. All ships of our own design. Two of them went out into the universe, spreading rumours of an answer to humanity's threat. Even before the destruction of Earth, we knew they would be their own demise and would not stop with their own world. They have always feared extinction. But when they faced it, they turned truly feral. Over the last hundred years, more people circulated the rumours and we have remained hidden in order to see our mission through. This is out headquarters. We call it *Haven*."

As they continued to watch on in awe, Jaxx noted a number of ships leaving the structure at high speed. The man beside them noticed it too, and his look became a grave one.

"What is it?" asked Quincy.

Chapter 6

"There's a battle nearby. That was the response fleet."

A whistling noise then encapsulated them all, forcing Jaxx to put his hands over his ears. Before his very eyes, the entire station of *Haven* vanished into nothingness.

"That's one hell of a cloaking technology you've got there uh…"

Jaxx chose that moment to realise he had not learned the man's name.

"Bingley. My name is Bingley."

Jaxx beamed a smile.

"Nice to put a name to the face. Now, just how many species do you have in the Unity?"

Bingley sat down on a nearby rock, and removed a tablet device from inside his jacket. With a few taps of his finger, a door previously hidden in the rock face opened, and a small scout ship became visible.

"The remaining few Saxons were the first to arrive, but we had scouts everywhere, and knew what they had done, so we locked them up straight away. Next to arrive were the Beresians, then the Janko decided that they were done aiding the humans. They helped us acquire the resources to build the docking ports and defence systems. And most recently, a small group of Valkor arrived from a distant system."

Jaxx's entire body went cold at the mentions of his species. He had believed he was the only one. That everyone else had been killed at the hands of the Decimators, or from the effects of their devastation. He never even considered some might have made it.

"You mean, there are more of my people on *Haven*?"

Bingley nodded and smiled. He could see his words had brought hope to this tall orange-skinned being.

"Two hundred, there or there abouts. And androids too."

He looked over at Quincy, who was now as astonished as Jaxx

was. Quincy knew there were others, but after his creator was killed and he was disassembled, he figured they had all been boxed up too. Bingley started walking towards the scout ship, and the others followed.

"We have over eight thousand people onboard *Haven*, and another thirty-thousand on the planet below. All kinds of species, all walks of life, all corners of the galaxy. We have been building this resistance for almost two centuries, and we are now finally reaching our pivotal moment. The Unity is strong, and we are ready to put an end to the human slaughter. Peace will prevail my new friends."

Although partially lost by the announcement that his species had survived even in small number, another nagging question burrowed its way into Jaxx's mind like a worm.

"If *Haven* is now cloaked, how are we supposed to fly into it?"

Bingley began chuckling to himself, shaking his head, clearly the only person in on a joke nobody else yet knew. Jaxx turned to Quincy.

"What's he laughing at?"

Quincy simply shrugged his shoulders.

"We aren't going to *Haven* my friends."

Jaxx and Quincy exchanged blank expressions once more before Bingley offered the answer they were looking for, but perhaps were hoping not to hear.

"We are going to the battle."

7

Despite multiple failed interrogation techniques, and the slowly melting sections of his mind, Jack Slater had finally managed to secure a location for the supposed organisation known only as 'The Unity.' However, in the extended time it had taken him and his crew to procure this information, several of them had succumbed to the in-built default that existed within each of them. Slater had been forced to personally extinguish the lives of thirty-four of his officers, with several others refusing to do it for him out of some misguided level of loyalty.

They all knew what they were. They knew they were clones of human ancestors. They knew they were not the *real* thing. And yet they seemed to insist on mimicking them almost to perfection. For Slater, this was only a weakness. He was always of the opinion that original humanity was far too weak. Far too bullish for their capabilities. It had been almost a perverse pleasure of his to extinguish that troublesome ball of rock and water. This new version of humanity would not be so reckless, he thought. It would be free of the defects of the biological design and reign forever amongst the cosmos.

Of course, in his pursuit of such sovereignty, he and his people had become far worse than the humans they destroyed. They were indeed feared, but had garnered no respect, no solid territory and crucially, no answer to their rapidly declining health condition. Every species in the galaxy was rushing to become part of this 'Unity' to stand against Slater and the rest of the Decimators, but not him. If the rumours were true, then there were Saxon scientists in this place. Scientists who may have worked on the Resurrection Chambers. Scientists who may have an answer.

Unfortunately, in slaughtering his creators in order to be free from their rule, he had also destroyed any answers or potential solutions that the facility on Deltaria may have held. And that was Slater's biggest failure. In attempting to escape captivity, he and his people had acted rashly, recklessly, and destructively for their own personal gain.

Just like real humans.

His anguish would have to wait, however. They were about to go into battle with many different species, in the weakest state they had ever been in. Their flagship, which was simply called such, with no designation or identifier, was now down to a skeleton crew of just eighty people, and their fleet in its entirety was down to just six ships, five of which were here. One was ordered to stay away. Slater's mind may have been disintegrating, but he was still an intelligent and devious man. The sixth ship was heading out on a mission of its own. A mission that may bear some kind of fruit. Time would tell if this was the case, and following this battle, if there were any Decimators left to take advantage of it.

Then again, there was always his *other* plan.

Sirens began wailing around the ship, and Slater marched onto the bridge, which was now in somewhat of a disarray. Conduits were hanging from the ceiling above the tactical station, although the console was fully operational, and there were scorch marks on the walls and floor from a previous skirmish with the Beresian Defence Force. With limited crew and time, repairs had been confined to the absolutely necessary, omitting the aesthetic elements. Glancing around, Slater still did not understand the logic of the original clones who built these vessels. He glanced at the charred and solidified sections of the chosen floor surface.

"Who the fuck puts carpets on a battleship anyway?"

Slater was snapped out of his potential monologue on the furnishing of their vessels by his first officer. That should be said, his *new* first officer. The previous occupant of the role was now lying dead in a bio-bed, with a rifle bolt through his skull. Another case of merciful euthanasia from the Captain.

"Sir, there is a large fleet of vessels approaching."

Slater climbed the miniature staircase to his centrally located chair, and sat down, the leather squeaking loudly as he did so.

"How many ships?" he asked curtly, ignoring the stabbing pains in his temples. The taste of copper filled his mouth. The decline was now in its advanced stages. This was an all or nothing scenario now.

"Seventy-five vessels in total sir."

The words hung in the air for a few moments, while the rest of the bridge crew looked around for some kind of suggestion of retreat. They were no longer the militaristic and stern creatures they started out as. The loss and decline of so many of their number had broken many of their spirits, and some wanted to run away from the mildest of skirmishes. Captain Slater, however, would never turn away from a fight. Even in the face of certain death. His mind was locked in, and that meant his crew were going with him.

"Prepare all weapons. Ensure shields are at maximum, and I

want rotating frequencies. Do not let them get a shot in. Understood?"

The bewildered officer simply nodded, and turned back to his station. The next order was directed specifically at the tactical officer.

"And make sure to put extra effort into shielding the ventral sections. If there's even a chance that the Coben woman, or that Valkor are here, then let's not have a *Challenger* related embarrassment."

Another curt nod from a face with fear in their eyes. A series of beeps and acknowledgements around the room confirmed they were as ready as they were going to be. This was either going to be a massacre, or a valiant victory.

Despite all his bravado, at that exact moment, Slater was hoping there would be someone left alive to celebrate it.

8

"Where's the rest of them?"
While Narlia's question was a rather shattering break of the silence on the Allurian bridge, her question was being wondered by many others. Doctor Vaysa had put the majority of the crew to sleep given their violent nature, and in doing so had wondered if they had restricted their effectiveness. Standing alongside Molly and Fay'Lar at this moment in time, he felt that they perhaps had left too many Allurian clones awake.

"Surely there must be others," Molly responded.

"Undoubtedly," Fay'Lar replied. "Slater may be a human, but he is not stupid."

She felt Molly's eyes glaring at her to her left.

"Present company accepted, of course."

A wry smile spread across Molly's lips, and she looked out once more onto the viewscreen. Displayed ahead of them, were five Decimator ships. Their black, reflective surfaces, were now not as covert as they once were. There were missing deck plates, hull panels, and even several smaller hull breaches, seemingly still sealed off by energy fields. Clearly, they too were low on numbers, and the military mind within Fay'Lar determined Slater must be prioritising defence and weapons over remaining stealthy. The human clones had lived up to their namesakes, and decimated half of the galaxy. But this had clearly come at a cost. The consistent battling and skirmishes had likely accelerated the degenerative effects in the minds of Slater's crew, and now they were facing quite a battle.

"Lieutenant, scan the vicinity for any further vessels."

The Allurian officer at the helm, grunted a noise of acknowledgement, albeit a disgruntled one, and began scanning for other ships.

"No further ships of this design, Captain."

"Maybe this really is all that's left of them," Vaysa spoke, almost melancholy in his tone. Whilst he was certainly not advocating for these murderers, any loss of life to a physician was regrettable. Especially with such wasted potential.

"Even so, five ships against seventy-five?" Molly asked. "That's suicide in any scenario, surely?"

Whilst her knowledge of this time and the politics at the time of her entry into this universe were limited back then, ten years of becoming exactly the same sort of fighter and mercenary that her predecessor had been had shown her a few things. Decimators weren't stupid, they usually had a back up plan, and they never backed down from a fight. But even by that logic, a seventy ship swing was not a small disadvantage to Slater's men.

The seventy-five vessels of which Molly spoke, were comprised of multiple different species, some even Fay'Lar knew very little of. They had come across the fleet en route to where they believed 'The Unity' to be located, when all ships detected the arrival of the Decimator vessels into the system. After a brief and potentially hostile situation was resolved, the entirety of the fleet, with the

Chapter 8

exception of one scout ship, was turned around, and they made their stand at the edge of the system, near the twelfth planet. The lone scout ship was sent on autopilot to the proposed location of The Unity with a pre-programmed distress beacon. Looking at the opposition, Fay'Lar could not help but feel that had been a waste of time and resources.

She stepped down from the rear of the rectangular bridge, and walked around where the captain's chair had been. After detaining the more incoherent and dangerous Allurian clones, she had ripped the chair from its mount, and flushed it out of an airlock. Allurian captains liked to engage in their romantic lives in a display to the crew of their fertility and attraction. It was meant to assert dominance and confidence in the other officers. Fay'Lar, however, and most of the other non-Allurian people on board, decided that was disgusting, and a chair covered in multiple bodily fluids was not something she wanted on the bridge of what was now her ship. After a brief exchange between her and the former Allurian second officer about disrespecting culture and honourable leadership, she won over her point, and now stood in the place the chair used to reside, and glanced at the newly installed command panels either side of her.

"Open a channel to the lead ship."

It took Molly a few moments to realise that she had become the communications officer, and snapped to it.

"Oh shit, that's me. One second please."

Desperately trying to remember which letters were represented by which symbols in Allurian language, she punched in a few commands, and the beep of success echoed around the room. She couldn't help but smile and give her best bravado in her response.

"Channel is now open, Captain!"

Even Fay'Lar could not suppress a smile at her enthusiasm. She was glad she had been acquainted with the *real* Molly after the events of ten years prior. She had proven a valuable contact. But now, it was time to get down to business.

"Slater, this is Captain Fay'Lar of the Deltarian Military. You are trespassing in friendly territory, your ships look like shit, and I haven't had my breakfast yet, so shall we end this now?"

Narlia sniggered at the tactical station. She had always been fond of her father's former tactical officer. Her wit and humour always managed to cut through the crap. However, the levity was soon ended, when the face of Jack Slater appeared on the screen. It was not what she expected.

His face was white as the hull on a Beresian vessel, his eyes were sunken, with dark purple rings surrounding them, sweat covered his brow, and his hair was slicked back with just three strands cascading over his left eye. He was clearly in a tremendous amount of pain, as his teeth were gritted tightly and his entire form was shaking.

"Oh don't worry, Captain. I intend to destroy you very quickly. I don't have much time, and there are people I need to see."

Fay'Lar squinted at the image of Slater, trying to make out the shapes behind him. And then behind her, Doctor Vaysa gasped, and Molly followed suit. It was a pile. A pile of bodies.

Dead officers lay tangled amongst each other, stacked almost vertically up to a height of around six feet. They too were white-skinned, clammy and had the same purple rings around their eyes. But the blood. There was so much blood. Seemingly picking up on their diverted attention, Slater turned around to survey his work, and then looked back at the screen.

"Oh them? Yes well you see Captain, some of my crew were beginning to descend the staircase into the basement of madness. I felt it better to spare them from that. A few of them tried to resist, but they all were subdued in the end."

And there it was. The madness that lay within every clone that

Chapter 8

exited any version of the Resurrection Chamber, on full display for all to see. Slater had butchered his own crew, and was now driving the rest into their doom. And for what? Molly was wracking her brains trying to think of what possible reason Slater might be trying to reach The Unity. And then it hit her, and she couldn't stop herself from shouting it out loud.

"Saxons. There must be Saxons at this Unity place."

Flickers of recognition flared in Slater's sunken eyes as he focussed not on her words, but on Molly's face. And then the return of the devilish smile as he realised why he recognised her.

"Molly, Molly, Molly. How long has it been? Must have been a decade by now eh? You were a worthy opponent, but you lacked the edge, the finishing blow of a true warrior. Well, your copy did anyway. You know, she was so stupid and self involved, she actually thought her weapons development hundreds of years ago was responsible for Earth's destruction? And they say we are the insane clones around here."

Slater attempted a laugh, but it gave way to a violent cough, and when his eyes returned to the screen, there was a trickle of blood making its way from the corner of his mouth.

"You don't look so good, Slater," Fay'Lar retorted, holding her hand up for Molly to remain where she was, although she was now seething with rage. "In fact, you look like you need putting down."

Fay'Lar turned to Molly, drew a thumb across her throat, and Molly cut communications. She turned to Narlia, took a deep breath and spoke just one word.

"Fire."

9

The identification markers were bouncing around the panel like Christmas lights twinkling on and off. Jaxx was stunned by the sheer volume of them concentrated in one place. He was equally stunned by the lack of the Decimator identity markers on the screen. Quincy had remained silent. He may have just been a collection of nuts and bolts to some, but he had proven to be a loyal friend to Jaxx, and right now they had a shared discovery. There were more of both of their species. Clearly, Quincy was as stunned as Jaxx had been. But the moment he was told by Bingley about the upcoming battle, he switched back into his renegade mode, preparing for flying manoeuvres,, fancy shooting, and potentially hand to hand combat once more.

"Approaching the twelfth planet now," Jaxx indicated, pointing at the screen in front of him.

"Alia."

Bingley's voice was quieter than it had been. He was deep in thought too.

"Sorry?" Jaxx asked.

Bingley looked up at him.

"The twelfth planet. It's called Alia. It is my home."

Jaxx's shoulders sank. Whilst the battle was happening in orbit, there was a strong danger to anyone living on the planet below. Bingley may have family down there, and he was very obviously worried for their safety. Jaxx knew what it was like to lose your home and your people, and while this was not a direct attack on Bingley's world, Jaxx knew that if it proved to be an advantage, Slater would target that world without hesitation.

"Well that just gives me another reason to kick some Decimator ass then, doesn't it."

He winked at Bingley, who could not help but smile. He leaned forwards and slipped into the weapons seat, and began tapping commands into the control panel. He glanced over at Jaxx.

"I will show you where the Valkor are living when we are all safe. They decided not to remain on board *Haven*."

Jaxx looked round at him, as he began to slow the ship down.

"Where are they?" he asked, now concerned he would have another quest to find his people. Bingley held up his hand apologetically.

"They decided to live on the planet below. There was a section of desert there, and they wanted to build their own home. To try and reconstruct a section of their homeworld to make their own. It's called New Arizona."

A newfound joy burst through Jaxx's heart and he grinned from ear to ear. He nodded thanks towards Bingley, and as the fleet of ships came into view, he altered course to approach from the side, putting his flight path directly between the Decimator vessels and the fleet.

"What are you doing?" Bingley asked.

"Flanking them," Jaxx replied. "They'll be so fixated on the seventy-five ships in front of them, they won't even bat an eyelid at us."

"You sound like you've had a lot of practice at this."

Jaxx rubbed the back of his dark orange neck with a shovel-sized hand, and shrank back a little.

"Some… not a lot."

Bingley laughed out loud, and punched more commands into his station.

"Weapons online and all disruptors are loaded. Ready when you are, my friend."

Jaxx nodded and hit the throttle, and the scout ship lurched forward, heading right for the side of the lead Decimator ship, which he assumed to be Slater's. Without breaking his gaze ahead, he leaned towards Bingley, and spoke in an authoritative manner.

"When I reach two-hundred thousand kilometres, I want you to target your disruptor fire at the larger hull breach on the starboard side. Understood?"

Jaxx received no reply.

"Bingley? You with me buddy?"

As Jaxx turned towards his co-pilot, his eyes bulged in horror. Bingley was dangling in the air, feet convulsing beneath him, blood pouring from his mouth…

…and Quincy's arm protruding through his chest.

10

"Where are those shields?" screamed Fay'Lar as the Allurian ship they had commandeered rocked violently from a torpedo blast.

"I don't know what happened!" shouted Narlia over the deafening sound of the claxons echoing around the bridge. "Whatever is in those torpedoes just cut right through our shields!"

Molly was struggling to stay in her seat at the communications station, but she was determined to decipher whatever was now coming through on a secure channel. Another hit, and the science console on the far side of the bridge exploded in a mass of shattered glass, splintered wires, and fire. There was no need to check on the condition of the Allurian crewman. The blood pooling around his body made that clear. And then the message became clear, and Molly's face turned a ghostly white. A change which Doctor Vaysa noticed.

"Molly, is everything okay?" he asked, fully aware that it was not okay at all. But his doctor's empathy insisted he try to comfort her whatever the news was.

"They're under attack," she muttered.

"Who's under attack?" the Doctor asked.

There was a moment of silence from Molly, despite the noise that was going on around her, everything was mute to her. Then she finally managed to get the words out.

"The Unity."

Molly knew the words had hit home with him, when she saw his face change colour despite its crystalline structure. There was no time to dwell on the assimilation of this information, as another hit struck the ship. The entire wall of consoles from the previously destroyed science station, in sequence, one by one, blew out with such force that every person stationed in front of them was effectively torn to shreds. Seeing the cascade coming, Vaysa threw Molly to the ground, but he was not fast enough to save himself. The communications console exploded directly into his face, tearing it clean off, and taking most of the front of his skin with it. While the death was instant for him, as his body landed next to Molly on the deck, it continued to twitch for several seconds before succumbing to its injuries.

She tried to scream, but wasn't sure if anything audible had made it out. That was when she felt Narlia's arm around hers, dragging her up to her feet. Vague words floating in the air amongst the muted sounds including 'abandon ship' made it to her ears. Molly managed to glance at one of the few remaining consoles as she was dragged into the emergency elevator shaft, and saw of the seventy-five ships they had begun with, only forty-two now remained. They had, it seems, vastly underestimated the power at Slater's disposal.

As the doors began to close, Fay'Lar leapt between them, a sizeable burn down the left side of her face, just as the entire viewscreen exploded inwards, revealing open space onto the bridge. Immediately, the vacuum effect took hold and sucked all of the debris and damaged ship components into space along with the bodies of the Allurian officers, and Doctor Vaysa. They had lost their captured ship, and now Fay'Lar would find herself in an escape pod for the second time in as many weeks.

Molly, however, was still focussed on the distress call she had intercepted before Vaysa had been killed.

'This is the Unity station Haven. We are under attack from friendly fire. The androids… they have gone rogue. Several hundred dead… key systems destroyed… orbit decaying… send help… please…'

11

"The fleet are attempting to retreat Captain."

Slater could not help but show a wild grin at the sound of his only surviving officer's statement. He had known they would underestimate the power of his ships. They were so confident that they came in large numbers to face just five vessels in opposition. And look where that had led them. Decimated.

"News from our allies?" Slater asked, the endorphins rushing through his body keeping the majority of the pain away for now.

"The androids are on the offensive. We now have an exact location for the *Haven* space station, Sir."

Without any sense that it was coming, Slater let out a full belly laugh, intermixed with coughing and spluttering. He had known the plan had been likely of success. The little breadcrumbs the humans and their ilk couldn't resist. Plans on plans and deception after deception had all been carefully planned out for a very long time. He had deliberately left that colony of Valkor alive when their home planet was destroyed. He *planted* those androids all over the galaxy at strategic locations where he knew they would be found. After all, he was the one who had shut them all down. Torath had long thought he was in charge. The so-called creator of the Decimators. But what he had really achieved was a concentrated purity of efficiency, and released it into the universe. Torath had never been in charge. He was obsolete the day Slater stepped out of the first tube. The Saxons were another species who had failed to recognise their own stupidity. Each time a clone failed to live the expected length of time, they would integrate the memories of that individual into the next one, and the next, and so on and so forth. This meant that when Slater had gotten to what was now his fifth incarnation, he had seen how cruel the Saxons were to them, how they were planned to be nothing more than foot-soldiers for them. By giving them the amalgamation of past memories, the Saxons had given the Decimators exactly what they had needed.

A motive.

Slater had known that the Valkor would seek out a similar world to theirs, and they knew they'd likely find it on the edge of known space. He had also known that the androids would be found en route to this place either by the Valkor, or other species chasing this fabled Unity. The only thing he had not known, was its exact location. Having cloaked vessels was one thing, but having a truly invisible sixth ship was another. The secret mission Slater had dispatched that vessel on, being the only one modified with such technology, was to follow the communications signals in the system, and pinpoint their source. It had travelled undetected and witnessed the station cloaking upon arrival. Then it was simply a matter of tapping into the scout ship audio to determine Quincy was indeed aboard, and through conversation, determine the other androids were being sheltered by The Unity. After that, it was merely the case of transmitting the activation sequence.

The modified weaponry including the transphasic torpedoes

that Slater had 'procured' from the Janko were simply a knife cutting through butter. Experimental technology was always something Slater had enjoyed testing, and with virtually nothing to lose in a final confrontation, he stole it, murdered the entire Janko colony, and headed out to meet a very underprepared resistance.

"Captain," the officer announced. "The fleet is down to twenty-seven ships, and they are heading towards the *Haven* station."

Slater nodded, and wiped the back of his hand across his brow to clear the cold sweat forming above his eyes.

"Set a pursuit course."

12

The weapons console exploded into shards of glass and vibrant orange sparks arcing through the air as Quincy's arm slammed into it with force. Jaxx threw himself against the bulkhead, grasping for anything he could find to defend himself. Even now, his eyes kept darting back to the slumped figure of Bingley, eyes wide open, face etched in shock, staring directly at him.

"Quincy what the fuck are you doing? It's me!"

Jaxx's pleas went unheard. The now dark glow from his friend's eyes was far from the friendly cobalt blue he was used to. There was no emotion on the android's face. It was completely blank and unresponsive to Jaxx's words. As Quincy swung his arm again, Jaxx ducked and rolled across the deck plate, the android's arm leaving a sizeable dent in the wall, the sound of the impact echoing around the entire ship. Jaxx's back rolled up against a medium sized cabinet that he had not noticed before. He tried to scramble to his feet, but Quincy was too fast. Before he could get to even one knee, Quincy grabbed him by the scruff of his shirt, lifted him clean off the ground, and threw him across the cockpit of the ship, where he smashed into the wall, glass falling all around him, and he landed behind an examination table in a heap.

As he looked up, his eyes trying to focus, he saw a very familiar weapon taped to the underside of the table, and could not help but smile to himself.

"What goes around comes around," he muttered to himself.

As Quincy stomped his way towards his former friend, Jaxx grabbed the Beresian disruptor, checked the charge and bathed in the comfort of familiarity. And just as he had done ten years previously in the bar where he first met Molly, he slipped into his old self again.

"So Quincy, were you waiting until we were officially a space adventuring couple before you told me you were a psychopathic vending machine? Or were you hoping to save it until after the wedding?"

Amazingly, the sarcastic venom caused Quincy to stop in his tracks for a moment, as if he was trying desperately to compute something. His eyes flickered between the crimson they had become, and the blue of the Quincy Jaxx had known all this time. Taking the chance, Jaxx swung up from behind the table, charged the disruptor and aimed at his friend. But when he saw the inner conflict going on, he paused.

"Quincy? Can you hear me?" he asked tentatively.

"Jaxx… you are… my friend…"

Jaxx's body felt a long and cold shiver run down its spine. And his eyes snapped into focus and realisation. *A signal.* Quincy was being influenced by an outside signal.

"That's right buddy. I know you love a good sarcastic comeback as much as the next guy, but right now I need you to be real with me. Whatever is trying to make you hurt me, I need you to fight it."

Chapter 12

The switching between red and blue in the android's eyes was now so intense it was almost like a rapid fire tennis match going on. Quincy's face now began to contort.

"Signal… ship… nearby… cloaked… Slater…"

A ship. There was a ship out there. Jaxx had to find it, but this scout ship was only designed for short range flight and minimal combat. There was no voice activation, and Quincy was standing next to the operations console. There was nothing for it. He knew he could repair his friend with only minor damage, and he couldn't take the risk that he wouldn't relapse. Quincy jerked back slightly as the battle in his neural net continued. And then his eyes turned solid blue. He looked at Jaxx with confusion and recognition in the same moment.

"Jaxx?" he asked cautiously.

"Yeah it's me buddy."

"Jaxx, I…"

Jaxx switched the disruptor to stun.

"I'm sorry Quincy, but I need to be sure."

Jaxx pulled the trigger and a yellow beam of energy burst from the tip of the rifle, striking the android directly in the centre of his chest. A brief look of shock flashed across Quincy's face, as his external flesh burned away like seared meat, before he fell back onto the floor, landing perfectly flat and with a heavy thud.

Jaxx took a deep breath and lowered the disruptor, before moving between the body of his former captor, and the hopefully only slightly damaged body of his friend, and slumped into the seat before scanning the nearby vicinity. No ships were detected, but Jaxx knew there was *something* out there.

"Think, Jaxx, think…" he kept repeating to himself, tapping his temple with the end of the disruptor.

"Plasma!" he exclaimed, throwing the disruptor to the floor. "If I vent the engine plasma, it'll be attracted to the tachyons present in a cloaking shield! Man if I had brains like this all the time, I really would be dangerous."

Several taps into the console later, and a white and silver trail began to flow from both of the scout ships engines out into space. Jaxx watched through the window as the straight line trajectory of the plasma began to swerve to starboard. And there it was. Moving slowly off the starboard bow was now a white and silver outline of a fairly small Decimator scout ship. Despite them being revealed, the ship did not alter course or attempt to defend itself.

"They don't know I can see them," Jaxx realised. "Time to find out exactly what weapons we have on this thing."

Jaxx leapt over to the weapons console, or what was left of it, and managed to reroute the commands back to the operations station. Not an ideal fix as now he had no control over scanners or any potential parlour tricks, but at this point he had to take what he could get. The inventory displayed to him revealed he had surprisingly powerful disruptor cannons mounted on either side of the ship, and a compliment of twenty-five torpedoes.

"Man, if this is a lightly armed ship, what the hell are their battleships carrying?" Jaxx said to himself in disbelief.

He moved the targeting scanners over the rear of the vessel and targeted their engines. He called up both disruptor cannons and prepped five torpedoes. He then took one glance over at Bingley, and then another down to look at Quincy on the deck beside him. His hand hovered over the console as he returned his gaze to the Decimator ship, rage billowing within him.

"Go fuck yourself."

Jaxx plunged his hand onto the 'fire' button and a barrage of energy beams and torpedoes careered through open space until they met the hull of the Decimator scout ship. The disruptor hits knocked the ship slightly off course, and as the five torpedoes hit, the engines ignited, and small ruptures began forming all along the hull, illuminated by matching explosions. Clearly this vessel was meant for covert operations only, because the cascading effect of the damage spread quickly. Within five seconds of the final torpedo's impact, the Decimator vessel erupted into a giant red and white fireball, sections of debris flying in every direction. And then all was silent and the black of space returned once more.

Jaxx felt relief wash over him, and he exhaled a deep breath he did not even realise he had been holding. And then he received two alerts simultaneously. Both were coming from the now reduced operations panel. Making quick adjustments, Jaxx minimised the weapons controls and returned to ops just in time to see not one, but two distress calls coming in on emergency channels.

"Oh shit."

The first one was from *Haven*.

The second one was from a fleet of damaged ships claiming to have been attacked by Decimator forces. But it wasn't the call itself that shook Jaxx. It was the voice of the person who sent it.

It was Molly's voice.

13

Thankfully, the focus on destroying what was left of their larger ships by Slater and his fleet, had given the smaller ships time to collect most of the escape pods, and now Fay'Lar, Molly, Narlia and the other survivors were now on the bridge of an unfamiliar vessel. The design, however, was stunning.

A sapphire blue wall surrounded what they assumed was the bridge of the vessel, the floor completely transparent. The sensation of standing over open space was incredibly surreal for the group as they stepped onto it, but the real impact was the temperature. It was hot as a desert here. Deltarians were used to heat, but this was next level. Fay'Lar, however, continued forward to speak to the Captain. Molly was the one with the problem.

The Captain of this vessel, was severely injured, blood pouring from his forehead and trailing over his skin. His *orange* skin.

The Captain, was a Valkor.

"Captain Fay'Lar, welcome aboard the *Sapphire Serpent*. I only wish it was under better circumstances."

The name of the vessel ringed a somewhat familiar bell for

Molly, but she couldn't place it. The dedication plaque on the wall nearby, however, cleared that right up.

'Sapphire Serpent. Registry VK-2025. Commissioned in honour of the legendary Earth vessel 'The Sapphire Serpent' which was believed to stalk the oceans and rumoured to be cursed by a vengeful spirit. We sail the stars as they once sailed the waters.'

Molly tuned back into the conversation in time to hear the Captain's brief summary of their survival and search for a new home. Her mind now floated to one person in particular. Jaxx. Was he here too? He had to be. From the personal logs of her former clone, she knew that he liked to insert himself wherever there was trouble brewing, and this was about to be the biggest conflict in recent memory.

"Captain Ezio, you need medical attention. Do you still have medical staff?"

Fay'Lar's attention to others and their wounds made Molly smile. She was completely ignoring the fact that half of her own face was burnt and likely beyond salvation. She had certainly changed in the last decade. But right now, the focus was on the battle ahead. They had survived the first wave, but this was far from over. As Fay'Lar relieved Captain Ezio from command and sent him and his injured crew to the medical bay, Molly this time took her station at the tactical console. Narlia's left arm had been caught by a minor explosion in the first attack, and so the two of them switched places.

"All stations, I need an immediate report on…"

"CAPTAIN!" one of the Valkor officers shouted interrupting Fay'Lar's command.

"Yes Commander?"

But the officer did not respond. He simply nodded towards the viewscreen. It then became immediately apparent that they had just lost the war.

Chapter 13

"My God."

Displayed before them was an enhanced image. An image of a gigantic structure breaking apart. The object itself must have been the size of two Deltarian cities combined, and the number of destroyed ships breaking away was in the thousands. Fire and repeated explosions ripped throughout blowing out airlocks, windows, hull panels until eventually the entire station broke into two halves. As the lower half erupted into a cascade of explosions, fire, and shattered debris, the shockwave from this event blew the top half of the station into freefall.

As the crew watched on, *Haven* fell from the sky and hurtled toward the planet below. It was too late.

Haven was destroyed.

The Unity was gone.

Slater had won.

14

It had been several hours since *Haven* had fallen from the sky. Debris still littered the orbit of the planet, and the impact zone on the surface was visible from the view screen and windows of every one of the surviving vessels under Fay'Lar's overall command. Escape pods and shuttles had been sent down to the surface immediately to search for survivors. There had been almost one-thousand-five-hundred Valkor living on the planet below. The station itself had, once final data was retrieved from the wreckage, in fact been occupying a population of twelve-thousand-fifty-two.

The shuttles returned with thirty-two survivors.

For the first hour after the rescue attempt, the remaining ships of the fleet had reinforced their shielding, attempted emergency repairs, prepped whatever weapons they had left in readiness for Slater's expected attack. But he never came. Molly had seen the condition he had been in before the first assault, and in truth, she suspected he had died since. But then again, he was too smart and too psychotic to not have a plan in place for his eventual demise. And that was a fear shared by the entire crew.

"Bridge to MedBay," Fay'Lar's voice cut through the hushed tones around the room. "Report on the crew's injuries please."

It was almost twenty seconds of dead air before the full report came back to her.

"Final report, Captain Ezio is dead. The First Officer is dead. The Chief of Security is in critical condition, and not expected to survive. The Communications Chief is dead. We have forty-one civilian casualties from the families on board, and four of those rescued from the planet have succumbed to their injuries. MedBay out."

The silence on the bridge was almost touchable. It hung heavy in the air like a thick cloud of death and smoke, threatening to choke the remaining life from all those on board. With Narlia undergoing reconstructive surgery on her arm, just Molly and Fay'Lar remained of the original crew on the bridge. And for the first time, Fay'Lar was lost. All those deaths, and ships lost. The sanctuary they had been seeking was gone along with all but the now reduced count of twenty-eight survivors. And the Decimators were still out there somewhere. And the worst part was, they had no idea where.

Until they did.

The effect of decompression on the humanoid body is quite distinct. But on the body of a Deltarian, the build up of ice on the outer skin almost turns their body into a glimmering mineral from a distance. The sight of the entire front of the bridge being blown away before her eyes filled Molly with both horror and wonder. The second or so where time seemed to stand still before moving in slow motion. She saw Fay'Lar's body ripped out into the cold vacuum, a look of surprise forever etched onto her face. The Valkor officers who were still alive at the time, almost cartwheeled out of the ship, and as Molly realised she too was next, she took the

Chapter 14

deepest breath she could and felt the cold surround her as she closed her eyes.

The movement was a sudden jerk, which almost caused her to release her tightly held breath, but then it moved into a silky smooth and ice cold blanket, guiding her away from the shell of the ship. Her hearing began to sound muffled, but she could hear random pop, pop, pop of explosions all around her, and forced her eyes to open in time to see the *Sapphire Serpent* blown apart with all those on board.

Every. Single. Ship.

Gone.

As the ice began to expand in her veins, and her life began to drain away, Molly watched as the five Decimator ships accelerated away from the destruction. It was over. They had failed to stop Jack Slater and his maniacal plans. Fay'Lar was dead. Narlia was dead. They were all dead. *Decimated.*

Molly finally closed her eyes and let out her last breath, and as her body froze in an almost serene position, her skin faded to white, and her heart stopped beating.

15

As her eyes bolted open, her lungs grasped wildly for as much oxygen as they could consume, and the sheer panic overtook every fibre in her body. She felt hands trying to keep her down, but her mind was racing with images that she couldn't comprehend. Flashes of a dark place filled with evil. More images of a beautiful forest, a waterfall, and several settlements. And angels. She had seen angels.

But now, as Molly knelt forward on the cold metal floor, trying to catch her breath, all of those images disappeared. Her eyes began to focus, and her breathing began to steady itself. She remembered watching her friend die. She remembered the feeling of being pulled into open space. She was still numb both in feeling and in actual touch. She tried to stand, but her legs were too weak, and she fell back towards the floor, but someone caught her.

Molly stopped trying to move, and simply moved her eyes up the hands of the person who had caught her. When the skin became visible over the top of the gloves she had been looking at, she knew who it was. Orange skin wasn't exactly a regular occurrence in this galaxy. As Molly's eyes met the glowing white of Jaxx's eyes, she knew she should feel some degree of anger. She had seen him kill her clone, and had almost felt the impact of the blade herself. But after ten years, she knew he had done the right thing. She had seen the damage the Resurrection technology had caused, the amount of bootlegged attempts to recreate it such as the one used by the Allurians. The sheer madness displayed by Slater was clear for everyone to see. And so she couldn't feel anger towards him. She felt relief. She felt like she was no longer alone. And so she hugged him tightly.

"Uh… good to see you too, I guess."

Jaxx had never been good in emotional situations. His own emotions usually led him down a path of regrets, but here and now, he just felt warmth. This was not the Molly he had known. She was gone. This was a totally different person, and she had done him no wrong. Perhaps that's why he had chosen to save her instead of Fay'Lar. He had seen them both drifting towards the planet, but had chosen Molly. She moved away, now able to stand on her own two feet.

"Thank you," she whispered, her voice cracking.

"You're welcome. I'm sorry I arrived too late. I had been having issues of my own."

Jaxx turned away and gestured to the far corner of the cockpit, where Molly could make out a blood stained sheet over a body, and what looked like a second body with metal protruding from a hole in its chest.

"Is that…" Molly started.

Jaxx nodded and his face filled with sadness as he stared at Quincy lying on the floor.

"An android. Yeah. His name was Quincy. He was my friend. When Slater's code invaded his systems like a virus, I had to take him down. I figured a high stun setting would disable him enough for me to fix him later. But of course the Decimators leave no survivors do they? The virus was designed to terminate all android neural activity at the first sign of tampering. He's gone."

Molly reached out and placed a cold hand on Jaxx's arm.

"Along with everyone else."

Jaxx nodded, and placed his own hand on top of Molly's. They both felt a connection in that moment that Jaxx had felt with her clone, a decade ago. Familiar. Comfortable. For Molly, it was the sense that they were now both people out of place. Jaxx was once again the last of his kind, and Molly was back to being as alone as she was when all this began.

"So what do we do now?" asked Molly.

Jaxx shrugged his shoulders.

"Slater is gone, if he's even still alive. I've no idea what he does next. With the level of death and destruction he has spread across the galaxy, I don't see how there is anyone left to tangle with. It's the end of everything."

From the corridor beyond the cockpit, the two of them heard the heavy thump of metal under boots. *Large* boots. Unmistakeable footsteps echoed down the chamber, and Jaxx immediately reached for the Beresian Disruptor, Molly moving back behind him, having got no weapon within her reach.

"Oh I wouldn't say it's the end of everything, my old Valkor friend," spoke the booming voice as the figure turned the corridor. "Simply the end of this era."

Jaxx lowered the disruptor, and his face could not hold back the initial shock. His white eyes darted over the hulking jewel-encrusted skin before him in disbelief. And then the shock was replaced by a wide grin.

Syl'Va moved forward and gave Jaxx a bear hug, patting him on the back so hard that he swore he felt bones crack, but none of that mattered.

"How are you here?" Jaxx exclaimed, remembering seeing the clone of Molly seemingly vaporising him a decade ago.

It was then that he noticed a glowing green light in the corridor behind Syl'Va. The Deltarian noticed the glance, and smiled, gesturing towards it.

"Not everything in this universe can be explained by science, my friend. There are things that we need to talk about."

MOLLY, JAXX AND SYL'VA
WILL RETURN.

BONUS CONTENT

SALTAIR AND KRENIK'S DAY OFF

Saltair let out a deep sigh of impatience.

"Oh don't be so ridiculous, you cantankerous little midget! You know as well as I do that system is off limits."

Krenik slammed his fist down on the console, and immediately withdrew it in regret. After all, parts were becoming more and more expensive in an increasingly depleted galaxy.

"Then what do you suggest we do, Saltair? Hmm? Wait until there are no supply depots left? Nobody to trade with? The human Decimators are keeping our species alive as a whole because we serve them. You and me are simply freelancers. We provide no more use to them than a toothpick to clean the meat from their mouths."

Krenik did have a point. And their latest contract was not providing sustainable. Twenty clones of Molly Coben still remained, and yet they could find no trace of any of them. They had lost two weeks of time repairing the damage to their battered vessel after retrieving the last clone. Now they were low on funds, and resources.

Saltair had to concede that his pint-sized companion was likely right. To find valuables that nobody else had, they must travel to places nobody else would. Namely, Earth. Or whatever was left of it.

"Can you guarantee that this ship will be able to withstand the gravimetric forces in the Sol System? Because I was under the impression that your Janko bodge jobs were mostly tape and glue."

Krenik winced at the mocking of his abilities. But he had known Saltair for long enough, and was aware he was simply poking him to provoke a reaction.

"This ship would withstand a slingshot around a sun if needed! Besides, you're the navigator. Just scan for anomalies and go around them. Even your politically riddled mind should be able to handle that."

Saltair did enjoy this kind of banter with his associate. It reminded him of the days on his homeworld when he was running for office. The barbs and insults, the declarations of impunity and inexperience, whether true or not. It is part of the reason their operation worked so successfully. Although he had total faith that the skills of his Janko compatriot were of the highest level, he would never have said so out loud.

"I shall have to make a note of that in my log," he replied sarcastically. "That way, if I die, I can sue you."

Even Krenik couldn't hide a smile at that remark.

"Very well then. Set a course for the Sol System. Maximum velocity."

Saltair pulled himself up on his bed, the notification from Krenik having woken him up to say they were almost at Pluto. He ran his tendril like fingers over his face, and closed his ocean blue eyes for a moment. As he did so, the room seemed to fall a little darker. The same nightmares had plagued him once more. Saltair was a member of a species known as The Others. While not much was known about this race, Saltair had vivid memories of his homeworld, and indeed their origins. It was this that troubled him so much about returning to the Sol System. He had only been there once before, and it had nearly cost him his life. Nobody knew how old The Others were, and Saltair had never revealed his age to anyone, always replying to the question with the phrase, "older than you think."

Even Krenik was in the dark about Saltair's past. It was the year 2151 on the human calendar, when the Other had last been in this system. He had detected an energy signal that piqued his interest, and diverted to investigate. He had managed to pinpoint the location to a city in the northern hemisphere of Earth. However, just as he landed his ship, and slipped into a nearby river to avoid detection, the Decimators had attacked. The hull was breached, and his ship began to fill with water. Every system was compromised and the vessel began to fail. Saltair remembered the feeling of drowning all too well. It was this experience which plagued his nightmares. It was the only time he truly had come face to face with his mortality.

Ironically, the destruction of Earth had provided his escape. As the crust of the planet dissolved, the base of the river gave way, and Saltair's vessel fell through the crumbling planet, eventually reaching the other side, emerging back out into space. At the last minute, he had managed to engage containment procedures, and cloak the ship. But he had only just reached safe distance when the planet finally imploded, and the shockwave threw him and his ship across the system.

"Are you coming to the bridge or what?" shouted Krenik over the comms. "You're meant to be steering this rig, remember?"

Saltair chuckled to himself briefly, before responding.

"I'm coming, I'm coming. Keep your overalls on."

The view had not altered in the vast time since Earth's destruction. There was less debris in the darkness of space, but plenty to identify the planets which previously occupied the system. Earth's destruction had had devastating consequences for the Sol System. The shockwave alone had caused the destruction of Luna, Earth's moon, and the changes in gravitational forces had sent Mercury into the Sun, Venus soaring out of the system, and Mars crashing into Jupiter causing an explosion of biblical proportions. The remaining planets simply floated aimlessly, spinning on their axis, devoid of all life. And yet it was humanity of which there was the greatest evidence.

"I'm reading large amounts of gold, silver, and platinum surrounding Earth's previous location, as well as dense concentrations of nitrogen and hydrogen. The latter two should help recharge our power cells for a year."

Saltair nodded, as he carefully navigated the instabilities and pockets of dense gravity. Just a single micron into one of those wells would crush their ship and they would become nothing but another piece of space trash in a field of endless debris.

"I've also got vast deposits of Branasium and Klamarite at Mars' location."

That caught Saltair's attention.

"How much?"

Krenik smiled wide enough to show off all of his black teeth. It almost gave his mottled grey skin a hint of colour.

"Enough to retire on."

Those two minerals alone were worth infinite amounts of credits to races such as the Allurians and Beresians. Their purity would be the deciding factor of course, but even with refinement, they could finally retire from this life, and find a quiet corner of the galaxy to hide in, away from the Decimators.

"How will we go about collecting that much Branasium? We don't have enough containment barrels," Saltair pointed out.

Krenik's smile did not waver.

"We don't," he answered coyly. "But they do."

A small display beside the gravimetric pockets on the navigational console lit up, showing the outline of a seemingly abandoned ship. It's construction was unknown to them, but sensors showed they appeared to be a cargo vessel. The hold was filled with containment units, and more than enough space to contain both valuable elements.

"Any lifesigns?" Saltair asked, already knowing that his mind was made up.

"None. If there were people on board, they're long dead. I'm just staggered the ship hasn't floated into one of these anomalies and gotten squashed."

"As am I, my Janko friend. Plotting a course now."

As Saltair and Krenik's vessel slowly made it's way towards the adrift vessel, the shimmer of light from the sun across the hull revealed something clinging to the side of the ship. Completely unaware they had a passenger, the partners sailed into the unknown.

To be continued…

DAVID W. ADAMS

Saltair and Krenik's Day Off will continue in
the extended version of *Resurrection: Dark Rising.*

ACKNOWLEDGMENTS

I have, over the years, thanked many people from all aspects and avenues of my life in the backs of my books. Sometimes, even mentioning famous people who have inspired me, despite I knew all too well that they would never see it. But, it was my book and I could say what I wanted to!

Now the series is coming to an end, I would like to unify my acknowledgements across the board into this one message. Particularly as I have even more people to thank years after the first book hit websites!

First and foremost, I must thank my incredible wife, Charlotte. Without her, I simply do not know where I would be, not just with my writing but in my life. I was starting to give up on almost everything when I met her, and she quickly became my rock, my confidante, and more importantly, my best friend. It is with her that I was able to start a family, and in February 2022, we welcomed little Molly Rose Adams into the world. They are both my world, and entire universe and I simply cannot imagine anywhere in the multiverse where we aren't all together.

Naturally, the next in line for thanks and appreciation would be my parents, Shirley and Vince Adams. Particularly since my introduction to various forms of social media in the last few years, I have come across far too many stories of unhappy childhoods, and lack of support from families of many people in my life. I, fortunately, am certainly not one of them. My mother and father have never once put me down, attempted to dissuade me from doing anything or making any significant life changes. They have shown me nothing but unconditional love, support, and at times, financial help. They continue to be a beacon of light in my life, and are devoted to my little family completely. If there was a blueprint on how to parent a child, these two would have written it.

That support flows down the family chain, and emanates from my sister, Francesca too. When we were younger, we did not get on. Always hitting each other, shouting at each other, and making each other unhappy and angry almost every day. But as we have gotten older, our bond has strengthened, and she has been there for me, Charlotte and Molly every step of the way. It has even reached the point where we left our home in Plymouth, and moved to Dorset, just a matter of streets away from each other! Her other half, Anthony, is a tower of strength for her, and their two children Jack and Isabelle are the jewels in their little family. It is a joy to be in their company, and their unique place on the autistic spectrum makes them extra loveable, and always fun to be around, because they adore companionship. I'm proud to be their uncle.

My grandparents played a vital role in my early life. My grandfather, William Henry Griffiths, for whom the first book is dedicated, was my best friend. I would see him every fortnight growing up, and he would always have a happy and yet powerful aura around him. He was a huge imposing figure in stature, but was as kind as could be. There were always miniature bars of chocolate in a tin waiting for me and Francesca, and a couple of quid pocket money. His death in 2005 devastated me, and in truth, 18 years later, still resonates within me. I miss him dearly.

My other grandparents, Marlene and Dave are a force of encouragement and love. Nobody fucks with my Nan. Not if they know what is good for them. I remember distinctly her glaring at my soon to be mother-in-law at our wedding when the registrar spoke the words 'if anyone knows of any reason why these two should not be married, speak now.' It was definitely a 'don't fuck with me' look. And of course my Grandad is nothing but a funny cuddle teddy bear, even now. His humour always cuts through any tension or discomfort, as bad as his jokes are, and I was proud to ask him to be my best man at my wedding, where he made the customary jokes, and I was blessed that he accepted.

I never had a job that I truly loved, until I moved to Ilfracombe in North Devon about a year and a half after my maternal grandfather died. I spent 10 months hunting for a job to no avail, before being told that whole time, the fruit and veg shop next door had been looking for someone! And so in the September of 2008, I began what would turn out to be 8 years working for the Norman family. That family made me feel like one of my own. I owe a debt of gratitude to Pam Norman for being my extra grandmother, Trevor and Sarah Norman for showing me such kindness, support and friendship, and Paula Hobman and her family for being like a crazy aunt and always cheering me up. I miss working for them, and being around them all the time, but they left an everlasting mark on my life that I will always carry with me.

Charlotte's Great Uncle Richard Oliver, and his daughter Nancy, have become two of our strongest connections. They have always backed us with whatever choices we made, and helped us along the way. They exude love and support, and at certain times, I'm not sure what we would have done without them. I simply cannot accurately place into words, what the two of them mean, but I like to think that they know.

And finally, I would like to take a minute or two to mention some of the people I have met in recent years through the wonders of the online community.

I joined Flare in 2023, a peer support group for those dealing with mental health issues and physical disabilities. It is a place to talk together, support others, and build a friendly safe community in the often toxic world of the internet. Founded by Robyn, Josh and Emma, it has gone from strength to strength and in doing so, I gained some very good friends. Like many friends, we have our differences, but the benefit they have given to my life has helped me develop my persona, particularly through their support of my social media presence and helping me to be more outgoing through mentoring and doing my own livestreams. Robyn in particular was instrumental in that, and for someone who has gone through so much in her short life, she gives so much more.

In the same timeframe, I met Chantel. Much like my Nan, you don't fuck with Chantel. She is fierce, devoted and loving in a way that makes her a very treasured individual. I have given her cause to digitally slap me in the face numerous times, but I have never stopped admiring her and the person she has become through the adversity she has battled through. I hope we remain friends for a long time to come.

BookTok's community changed me for the better. I met some wonderful author friends, and not only are they kind and supportive and funny, they are extremely talented writers and designers.

RD Baker is one of my closest author friends. Which is no mean feat considering she lives in Australia! I had never read either a fantasy or spicy book until I was enraptured by her book *Shadow and the Draw*. The world building was so well done and yet I was able to follow it all! I have since joined her ARC team and anticipate every book she writes with rising enthusiasm. She is also an incredible advocate for indie authors, and kindness across the world. If you haven't read her books before, what are you doing with your life?!?!

Next up is someone who I came across during a giveaway she was doing on TikTok. Alexia Mulle-Rushbrook very kindly sent me a free copy of her dystopian sci-fi *The Minority Rule*, and once I read it, I immediately bought the rest of the trilogy, devouring each book. They were simply wonderful, and I was happy to become part of her ARC team for the more recent release *They Call Me Angel*, which was her best work to date. She is a kind and giving person, and we chat often through direct messages, and always support each other on TikTok.

And no thanks would be complete without the presence of Christian Francis. I came across him when I saw one of his many videos on TikTok offering advice to indie authors like me, and everything the man said made perfect sense, and I followed it often. I particularly enjoyed his video on writing a scary scene which I may have coerced into a particular chapter of *Frame of Mind*, so this is me giving him credit! He also very kindly was the man behind this redesign of *The Dark Corner* series, and I will never forget the time, effort and resources he provided to me for that task. As if that wasn't enough, he designed the covers for my other series *The Frozen Planet Trilogy*, and created the amazing *myindiebookshelf.com* which champions indie authors, giving them a platform to showcase their work and link people exactly where to find them. And let's not forget that his books are fucking awesome. Disturbing… but fucking awesome.

Well, I have rambled on long enough. It's almost as if I was reciting my life story at times, I know, but with this being the best version of my work out there, I wanted to really get the message across.

Arnold Schwarzenegger says often that people are free to call him many things, but don't ever call him a self-made man. Because he has had help from people all his life, and without them, he wouldn't be who he is today. And that sums up perfectly how I feel. Without all the people I mentioned above, I wouldn't be who I am today.

I have written many books since my debut, and I am proud of most of them. While *The Dark Corner* series comes to an end, other journeys begin, and I am happy to say I don't see me stopping typing away anytime soon. So thank you for joining me on the journey, and I hope we can go on many more adventures together as the years go by.

Oh and one more thing…

It is possible to make no mistakes and still lose. That is not failure, that is life. I feel too many people forget that, particularly in this industry.

Take care, and see you in Sisko's.

David W. Adams
November 2023

ABOUT THE AUTHOR

David was born in 1988 in Wolverhampton, England. He spent most of his youth growing up in nearby Telford, where he attended the prestigious Thomas Telford School. However, unsure of which direction he wished his life to go in, he left higher education during sixth form, in order to get a job and pay his way. He has spent most of his life since, working in retail.

In 2007, following the death of his grandfather William Henry Griffiths a couple of years earlier, David's family relocated to the North Devon coastal town of Ilfracombe, where he got a job in local greengrocers, Normans Fruit & Veg as a general assistant, and spent 8 happy years there. In 2014, David met Charlotte, and in 2016, relocated to Plymouth to live with her as she continued her University studies.

In 2018, the pair were married, and currently reside on the Isle of Portland, Dorset.

The first published works of David's, was *The Dark Corner*. It was a compilation of short haunting stories which he wrote to help him escape the reality of the Coronavirus pandemic in early-mid 2020. However, it was not until January 2021, that he made the decision to publish.

From there... *The Dark Corner Literary Universe* was spawned....

You can follow David on TikTok @davidwadams.author.

tiktok.com/@davidwadams.author
amazon.com/stores/author/B08VHD911S

Milton Keynes UK
Ingram Content Group UK Ltd.
UKHW020105241124
451242UK00016BA/214/J